The Billionaire Falls

Billionaire Bachelors

Book Three

Melody Anne

DEDICATION

This book is dedicated to Loretta, who is one of the greatest people I know. Thank you so much for all the support you've given to me and for all the good times we had working together. I miss you more and more each day since you moved so far away.

Books by Melody Anne

*The Billionaire Wins the Game
*The Billionaire's Dance
*The Billionaire Falls
*The Billionaire's Marriage Proposal
*Blackmailing the Billionaire
*Runaway Heiress
*The Billionaire's Final Stand

+The Tycoon's Revenge
+The Tycoon's Vacation
+The Tycoon's Proposal

Midnight Fire - Rise of the Dark Angel – Book One
Midnight Moon – Rise of the Dark Angel – Book Two

See Melody on Facebook at facebook.com/authormelodyanne

Melody's web site at www.melodyanne.com

Twitter: @authmelodyanne

Note from the Author

This story was another turning point for me. I tend to love those very alpha guys with a heart of gold underneath, and that's how I planned on making Mark… But things don't always turn out as planned. Mark ended up having a much softer side. I don't want to give too much away.

Thank you to all those people who make these books work for countlessly reading and then re-reading my material, for offering advice, and for putting up with my midnight idea sessions.

Thank you to my family, who I couldn't do this without. My children are a blessing for me every day (well, they are teenagers, so we'll modify that to say most days) The Anderson children are very much mirrored after my two amazing nephews, who I adore beyond anything. Thank you to my sister and brother-in-law for Jacob and Isaiah, who I think are the two greatest kids in the world. I even managed to teach them to say "Auntie Mel" whenever I ask them "who's your favorite auntie?"

As always, thank you to my fans. You're amazing, and I can't wait each day to read your reviews and talk with you through all the social networking. As long as you keep asking for more, I'm more than happy to give it to you.

A big thanks to my husband, who has become an outstanding cook since I refuse to even enter the kitchen anymore. He thinks I've become surgically attached to my computer chair.
I hope you all enjoy the third book in the Anderson Series. Mark is pretty close to my heart.

Melody Anne

Prologue

Joseph Anderson sat back in his favorite chair, enjoying the taste of his sixty-four-year-old scotch and the warmth from the softly crackling fire. Full of great food and gratitude, he thought back over the wonderful Thanksgiving he had just celebrated with his family.

He loved it when they all gathered together. He was happy to have so many new grandkids to love and spoil — oh, how he loved being a grandfather. His youngest granddaughter, Katie, had just turned one year old a week ago. There was so much to be thankful for.

He just wished his youngest son, Mark, would find the right woman. Joseph's breath rushed out in frustration. He'd found a few suitable matches for his boy, but Mark was a sneaky one and had avoided all his attempts.

Joseph guessed Mark had figured him out. Joseph wasn't one to brag, but he had been successful in finding love matches for both Lucas and Alex. Their wives were amazing women, and even better, they'd brought him grandchildren to fill the tired old hallways of his home, which had seemed barren for so long.

Well, Mark had underestimated his father, because Joseph knew he'd find a bride who could lasso his son. Though his kid was stubborn, Joseph was even more so. He wouldn't rest until Mark was happily settled down.

Joseph suddenly heard a one-person stampede coming toward him down the hall. He'd know the sound of those little shoes anywhere.

"Grandpa, hurry up! Grandma says it's time for dessert," Jasmine, his oldest grandchild, said a little breathlessly. She had to have run the whole way — there was nothing like dessert to motivate a child.

Joseph put his drink down and held his arms out for his beautiful six-year-old granddaughter to jump into. "Well, I certainly wouldn't want to keep you waiting to have some pie," he said as he carried her from the room.

"I *know*," said Jasmine, because the matter was of the utmost importance.

"Let's go find everyone and eat some pumpkin pie," he said to Jasmine before tickling her tummy.

"Uncle Mark said you were probably up to no good," Jasmine said in a whisper, acting as if she were divulging a huge secret.

"Your Uncle Mark was right. I'm planning on him giving you some more cousins, but let's keep that between you and me."

"I promise," Jasmine said. She then held her hand up to "pinky swear" on the matter.

Joseph hugged her tightly before making his way to the rest of his family. He was truly a blessed man.

Chapter One

Emily was struggling not to fidget with the salt shaker and the ketchup, but her nerves were in rags and tatters. She was waiting for Joseph Anderson to meet her for an interview.

She'd spotted the help-wanted ad in the paper a week ago and called right away. There must have been a lot of applications, for she'd paced by the phone like a lovesick teenager, praying he would call, and she'd already given up by the time he finally did.

He'd asked her to meet him at the small diner in a tiny town not far from Seattle. She preferred life in the country to that in the big city, where, for her, getting lost was almost an everyday occurrence. She was down to her last few dollars and had to be out of her motel in two more days. She couldn't blow this job interview.

Mr. Anderson was looking for a live-in housekeeper and cook — free room and board! If she got the position, maybe she could finally give her son some stability. She cringed as she thought of the past year and all her son had been through.

Her husband had died in an ugly automobile accident. She'd already been planning to leave the serial louse, but the accident had left her and her world shaken. His incredibly wealthy parents had decided they were better suited to raising her son than she was.

She'd figured they were just grieving the loss of their only son and would soon back off. Then she'd been served with custody papers. When she read the name of the judge on the papers, she decided it was time to go on a long vacation.

Her ex-father-in-law and the judge were golfing buddies, and she knew if she set foot in that courtroom, she would walk out without her son. They knew she was too poor to hire an attorney to fight them, much less know how to request a new judge since it was obviously a conflict of interest. She'd taken all her savings and been on the run ever since. She simply didn't have the kind of money it took to fight her son's grandparents.

Her deceased husband had contrived to leave her and her son nothing, and she was fine with, that. She wanted nothing from that sad excuse for a human being. He'd been wrapped around his parents' fingers, and they'd taken everything from her when he died, even her car. She'd had to buy a beat-up Pontiac, and it had one foot in the grave.

She knew that his grandparents would have provided her son with far more than anything she could ever give him, but that meant nothing if he wasn't given love. So she'd ended up in the little community of Fall City, Washington, because her car had finally refused to go any farther, and she'd been staying at the small motel in town ever since.

She'd been trying desperately to find any kind of work when she'd spotted the ad in the paper for a cook and housekeeper. It was perfect. She could work full time and still be with her son. She hadn't exactly told her potential employer about Trevor, but if he hired her, he certainly couldn't fire her just because she had a son. That would be discrimination, wouldn't it?

Emily glanced nervously over at the booth across from her, where her son was sitting down. She'd bribed him with a huge ice cream and the promise of a movie at a nearby dollar theater later if he sat quietly while she had the interview.

Luckily for her, the waitress had given him a coloring book and crayons, so Emily could count on him being busy for hours. Trevor was a creative kid, always curious and happy with any project she put before him. It was very nice when they were trapped in small hotel rooms. At least he didn't get bored easily.

The chime of the door opening drew her attention away from her son. A very tall older man with twinkling blue eyes and what seemed like a permanent smile on his face walked through the door.

"Good afternoon, Joseph," the waitress said with genuine warmth.

Show time. Emily had an empty feeling in the pit of her stomach — stupid nerves. She glanced at

Trevor, making sure he was occupied, then stood and walked over to Joseph.

He spotted her and smiled. "You must be Emily," he said in the loudest voice she'd ever heard. She nodded at him and then took the hand he was offering.

"Did you already order something to eat?" he asked.

"No."

"Well, let's order some breakfast. We can chat while we're waiting for our food. Molly makes the best omelets in the entire state," he said as the waitress approached.

"Can I have some eggs, Mom?"

Emily was paralyzed for a moment. She hadn't wanted her prospective employer to know about Trevor until the job was hers, but she figured it was inevitable.

"I didn't know you had a son," Joseph said with the same twinkle in his eyes.

"I was going to tell you today," she said, looking down at the formica table.

"Of course you can have some eggs, young man. I see you're coloring over there. Why don't you grab your crayons and come sit here with us?" Joseph said.

Emily could tell he was a man used to being in control. She sighed inwardly and went with the flow, not wanting to contradict her potential boss while he was interviewing her. That was a sure way for her not to get the job.

Joseph decided to order for all of them. Emily began totaling the bill in her head, hoping the job came through because breakfast was going to eat up most of her cash.

"What is your name, boy?" Joseph asked kindly.

"My name is Trevor. I'm five years old," he stated proudly.

"Five is a wonderful age," Joseph said. Trevor beamed at him, and Emily could see a little bit of hero worship forming. Her son had never had a proper father figure.

Joseph turned his attention back to Emily. "We spoke only briefly on the phone, so let me tell you a bit about the position."

"That would be great," Emily said. She really didn't care what the position entailed. She would scrub out toilets or muck out stalls if it gave her son real stability.

"The position is for a housekeeper and cook, though more of a cook. There's a cleaning service that comes in regularly. The place is quite large and frankly too much for one person to handle. Can you cook well?" he asked.

"Yes, Mr. Anderson. I don't like to brag, but I have a passion for cooking and love to try new recipes. I can make just about anything and can easily cook for one or for a hundred," she said enthusiastically. Her husband had expected her to impress his parents' cronies and their children, and she was well-versed in the art of cooking a complicated meal. She missed being able to prepare a meal in a nice kitchen. Being on the run wasn't pleasant for Trevor or for her.

"I cooked in smaller restaurants when I was younger, but I have done many parties where I've prepared complicated meals. Unfortunately, I don't have any references, but if you show me to a kitchen, I would be more than happy to prepare any dish you'd like." She knew she sounded a little desperate, but she needed this job so much, and was terrified that it might slip right through her fingers.

"We'll get to that. I tend to have a gut feeling about people, and you seem like an honest gal. If you can't cook, we sure will find out quickly, won't we?" he said with a laugh.

"Yes, that's true," Emily answered, not knowing how else to reply.

"The position provides room and board, as well as a weekly paycheck. Are you willing to relocate?" he asked and then glanced at her son.

"We love this area so much and have been hoping to find a job so we can stay. Trevor's a really great kid, and you won't be able to tell he's around," she promised.

Joseph laughed aloud. "I have three boys of my own, and a ranch would be a great place for a kid. If no one knows he's around, that's the time to worry about what he's up to."

Emily wasn't sure whether he was saying her son would be welcomed or not. So she remained quiet and hoped the man liked children.

"Trevor, do you like animals?" Joseph asked.

Trevor tilted his head as he did when he was thinking deeply about something. "I really want a puppy," he finally said.

"Well, of course you do; all boys should have a lot of puppies," Joseph said. He spoke as if it were a matter of life and death.

All ranches had at least a dog or two, she was sure; her son would be in heaven. They continued to chat as they ate breakfast. Emily was surprised how good the food was. She knew her food, and the omelet was light and moist and the vegetables were cooked to crisp-tender perfection. She would have to thank the cook before leaving.

Breakfast lasted for about an hour. This was unlike any job interview Emily had ever had, and she was starting to worry. Joseph wasn't asking her much at all that was relevant to the position, or any of the usual questions prospective employers ask. He was far more concerned with her personal life. Luckily, nothing he asked was improper or would have required her to lie.

"What made you decide to relocate all the way up here?"

Surprise filled Emily when she actually found herself telling him. "I was married for six years to a man who… Well, it wasn't working out. About six months ago, he died in an automobile accident and I decided that it was time for Trevor and me to start afresh." She had to stop herself before she brought up the whole custody situation. The man hadn't asked for these particulars, but he inspired a person to tell him their life story.

Joseph paused as he seemed to assess her. Emily could feel a bead of sweat forming on her brow. She knew it would go against her to seem so desperate in a job interview, but she desperately needed the position. After this, she was pretty much out of options.

"Emily, I think you're a perfect fit. When can you start work?" Joseph finally asked her.

"I could start right away," she replied. Darn. She'd forgotten to hide her eagerness.

"Well, there's no time like the present. Let me take care of this bill, and you can follow me out to the ranch," he said as he stood up.

"I can pay for mine," she offered, not used to accepting handouts, even when she had nothing.

"Nonsense, my dear; this was my interview. Why don't you get your son and meet me out front?" he said. She could tell there would be no arguing and did as he asked.

"Where are you parked?" he asked her when he stepped out front.

"I'm staying at the motel down the street, but my car isn't working right now. I need to get it repaired." She blushed to admit how dire her circumstances were. She was hoping he wouldn't change his mind, thinking she was just too messed up at the moment to be in his employ.

"Well then, hop in my car, and we'll swing by your motel so you can gather your belongings and get checked out. I'm happy to give you a ride to the ranch. Is your car at the shop here in town?"

"Not yet. It's still at the hotel," she quietly replied.

"That's no problem. We'll have it towed there. The guys here in town do excellent work, and they can have it delivered when it's all done."

"Thank you," she said.

That ad in the paper had been a godsend. She hardly cared what the job entailed. She was excited to have a place to stay, and her first few paychecks would cover her car repairs. Life could start getting back to normal for her and Trevor. Better than normal since she was no longer with her controlling, cheating ex-husband.

Chapter Two

Emily didn't take long checking out of the motel. She didn't have much — mainly clothing and some of Trevor's favorite toys and books. She'd been in a hurry to pack up and leave her old home, and she knew possessions could easily be replaced but her son couldn't.

They were soon off and heading up a winding road, away from the small community. "The ranch house isn't too far from town. It's most definitely beautiful country out here," Joseph said.

"I agree. I can't believe I've never been out to this area," she responded.

"Where are you originally from?"

Emily didn't know whether to tell him the truth or not, but she knew that if she started building a huge story around herself, it would be difficult to keep it up. She decided it would be best to stick with the truth as much as possible.

"We're from the Los Angeles area. We got sick of the crowds and pollution and decided to drive north until we found somewhere we couldn't leave. It turned out Fall City became that place," she said.

"With a bit of help from your car breaking down?" he asked with a laugh.

"Yes, that was certainly a deciding factor. But, as it turns out, it was a great place for it to happen in. The people have been more than friendly here. I am glad to have discovered this very green and clean area. I think I can be happy here."

"That is because you have excellent taste, my dear," Joseph said.

Trevor's questions started to fly quick and fast, and Joseph happily answered them. Emily sat back and enjoyed the drive in the comfortable sedan.

"Are there kids to play with here?" Trevor asked anxiously.

"There are a lot of children in the area, Trevor. I think you will have so many friends, you won't know what to do with yourself," Joseph said.

"Yea. I miss my friends."

"A young lad such as yourself should have a lot of friends to play with. The ranch has all kinds of things for you to do, such as learning to ride horses, feeding the chickens, watching the tractors, and making forts in the barns," Joseph told him.

Trevor was bouncing in his seat, eager to arrive at this wonderland of fun.

They turned off the road and crossed under a huge sign saying *Three Sons Ranch*. The driveway was shaded on either side by huge oak trees that looked hundreds of years old.

Emily's view was blocked by all those leaves, and her anticipation grew.

"My great-great-grandfather built this ranch over a hundred years ago, with not a penny in his pocket. He loved the land and knew he could make something out of it. It's been passed down through the years. My beautiful wife, Katherine, and I have chosen to live in the city, but Mark has always been a country boy, so it belongs to him now. His brothers come up and help out whenever they want to get away, but no one loves it the way Mark does," Joseph told her.

Emily was shocked to find that Joseph wasn't going to be her employer. "You don't live here? I'm going to be working for your son?" she asked.

"Yes, you'll be working for Mark. He had to go to Montana for some ranch business and won't be back until next week. He asked me to deal with the hiring. Don't you worry, though. There is plenty of staff, so you won't be alone up here. All our employees are trustworthy and good people. You and your son will be more than safe," he assured her, misunderstanding her fear.

She wasn't worried about her safety. She was worried that her boss wasn't going to like having a five-year-old boy running around his ranch. She would have to make sure Trevor stayed out of Mark's way and behaved exceptionally well, which could be a tall order for a boy. But she figured they would be in a bunkhouse and never run into the boss.

Emily lost her breath as they rounded a corner and the house came into view. It was magnificent. She thought she'd seen wealth before, what with everything her ex-in-laws had, but it was nothing compared with what was in front of her.

The home was three stories high and seemed to stretch out forever. It was beautiful and not at all what she'd expected. When Joseph had said a ranch house, she'd envisioned a great little 1800s farmhouse with a wraparound porch. It definitely had a wraparound porch, but it was huge. There was a second-story balcony as well, with several different French doors allowing access to it.

"Wow, is this a hotel? Is there a swimming pool?" Trevor asked as they stepped from the vehicle.

Joseph chuckled. "No, it's the main house, Trevor. You and your mom will be living here, and yes, there's a pool you can use any time you want, but only if there's an adult to watch."

"OK," Trevor said and started running for the massive front doors.

"Trevor, wait for us, please," Emily called after him.

He stopped immediately and turned toward his mom, although he was practically dancing in place.

A door opened as they started up the stairs. "Hello, Mr. Anderson," an older gentleman said.

"Hello, Edward. How are you doing today?" Joseph asked.

"I can't complain," the man answered.

"Emily, this is Edward. He does a little bit of everything here. And Edward, this is Emily, the new cook. This strapping young man is her son, Trevor. They will be staying in the east wing. Can you show them to their rooms?" Joseph asked.

Emily missed the wink Joseph gave to Edward and the answering smile he gave back.

"It's great to meet you, Emily and Trevor. Follow me; I'm sure you're anxious to get settled in," Edward said.

"It's really nice to meet you, too. That sounds great," Emily responded.

"Where are the dogs?" Trevor asked.

"After you get unpacked, I'll take you out back, and you can meet Sassy. She had puppies a couple of weeks ago, and I'm sure they'd love to meet you," Joseph said.

"Come on, Mom. Hurry," Trevor said, grabbing her hand.

Emily laughed at the excitement shining in Trevor's eyes. She hoped her new boss was a good man, because showing this place to her son and then having it taken away from him would be far too cruel.

"I'm coming," she responded.

"I'll meet you downstairs in the den," Joseph said before heading off down a long hallway.

"This place is huge," Emily said as they followed Edward up a large staircase and down an even longer hallway.

"You'll get used to it in no time," the man responded with a kind smile.

Emily wasn't so sure but nodded at him anyway. Everywhere she looked there were priceless portraits and antiques. It was all very overwhelming.

"I know you weren't expecting two people, so Trevor and I can share a room. It's really no problem," she told him.

"Oh, there's no need for that. There are plenty of empty rooms in this old place just waiting to be occupied. The original house burned down long ago, but years later, Mark's granddad built this place, and then Mark updated it and added more square footage. He wanted plenty of room so his family would visit often. The Andersons value family and friends above all else," Edward said.

"Here's your room, young man," he said and opened a door. Trevor squealed as he ran inside and jumped onto the huge bed. The room was bigger than their old living room and dining room combined. "We didn't know we were going to have a child here, so we will furnish it more suitably for you over the next couple of weeks," Edward said.

"There's no need to do anything extra. This room is beyond fine," Emily quickly replied, awestruck at the room's size.

"Your room is right across the hallway," Edward said and opened the door for her. She actually gasped. It was even bigger than Trevor's room. There was a magnificent four-poster bed centered in the room and a huge window with a charming window seat. She'd never want to leave.

"You have a private bath through that door there. We'll have it fully stocked by the end of the day. Your closet is through the door over there. When you're ready, come downstairs and take the hallway Joseph took." He turned and left before Emily realized she hadn't even thanked him.

"Wow, Mom, your room is even bigger than mine. Ooh, you have a seat on your window," Trevor exclaimed as he came bounding in, and he headed straight for it. "Oh! Look at all the horses," he continued on.

Emily joined him and stared at the picture-perfect scene before her. Her bedroom view was the back of the property, with a pasture of at least a hundred horses grazing.

"Look, Mom, you can go outside right through here." Trevor opened French doors she hadn't even noticed and walked outside before she could gather her thoughts.

"Trevor, be careful," she said and rushed after him. She breathed a sigh of relief when she noted the railing around the balcony. Her son was safe. The balcony wrapped around the entire back of the house. She saw another set of doors and wondered where they led but didn't want to be nosy. It was probably another guest room or a hallway.

"Let's unpack our suitcases and then head back downstairs. We don't want to keep Mr. Anderson waiting on us," she finally said. "You have to remember that we are *working* for Mr. Anderson, Trevor. We aren't his guests, so you have to be on your best behavior at all times and stay out of stuff. Can you promise me to be good?"

Trevor looked at her with his huge, innocent blue eyes before nodding. The mischief lurking there didn't reassure her. She'd have to do her best to do her job while keeping a good eye on her son.

"I'll be good. Now, can I can see the puppies?" Trevor asked, before running back inside and zipping across the hall to his own room.

She quickly put her few things away and headed to Trevor's room, where he was cramming his clothes into the dresser. She liked to let him do things on his own, but she knew she would have to redo the clothes later.

Emily collected Trevor, and they began the journey back down the stairs and followed the hallway toward the sound of voices. She heard a loud laugh and stepped through a doorway into an inviting room. A warm fire blazed in the fireplace, and Joseph was sitting on a soft, overstuffed sofa.

The room might have come as a surprise to Emily, because it was set up far more for comfort than as a showpiece. But a similar taste guided the décor of the other parts of the house she'd seen so far. Expensive artifacts, displayed behind glass, provided focal points, and yet simple touches made it look homey and inviting. Fresh flowers were placed throughout, and the furniture wasn't something you'd be afraid — or unwilling — to sit on.

"There you are. Did you get settled in?" Joseph asked when he spotted them.

"Yes, we did. Thank you."

"Can we see the puppies now?" Trevor asked.

"Trevor, wait until Mr. Anderson offers," Emily admonished him.

"It's perfectly all right, Emily. I understand Trevor is excited. Let's go," he said and led Trevor from the room.

Emily followed them down the hallway into the kitchen. She stopped and looked around in complete rapture. It was the most heavenly kitchen she'd ever set foot in. There was every known gadget she could imagine. She completely forgot about the puppies as she wandered around the massive island, looking in the cupboards and the fully stocked commercial refrigerator.

She realized what she was doing and looked up guiltily at Edward, who was smiling from the doorway. "I'm so sorry. I shouldn't have started getting into things," she said with embarrassment.

"This is your area; I'm more than pleased to see you're happy with the accommodations. On average, you'll be cooking for about twenty men a day, five days a week. It can get a bit overwhelming."

"This kitchen is a dream come true. I love cooking for large crowds. Please tell me they like to try new things and not just beans and ham," she said.

Edward laughed out loud. "I think if you're doing the cooking, the men would eat worms."

"You're much too flattering," she said with a smile. Emily could tell she and Edward were going to be great friends.

"Why don't you spend as much time as you want in here and get comfortable with where things are? Your son is in puppy heaven right now and will be perfectly fine," he said before slipping out the door.

Emily walked over to the large patio door and spotted her son and Joseph sitting on the covered porch with six black Lab puppies crawling all over the both of them. Trevor threw his head back and laughed with pure joy as one of the puppies stretched out across his body and licked him right across the face.

It was apparent that her son was in good hands, so she headed back to the kitchen to explore. Taking inventory of what food was there, she found paper and a pen and began creating a menu for the next couple of days. She couldn't wait to start preparing a meal.

Emily looked up as her son and Joseph came back into the room and then noticed the clock. More than an hour had passed, and she hadn't checked on Trevor the whole time. She couldn't believe how secure she was already feeling in the new place.

"What do you think of your kitchen?" Joseph asked.

"Oh, it's absolutely perfect. I can't wait to get started on dinner."

"You don't have to start tonight, you know. You can wait until tomorrow."

"I don't mind starting tonight. I honestly love to cook, and this kitchen is more equipped than a five-star restaurant. My hands are itching to begin."

"Only if you insist. But I'll admit that the guys would much rather have a home-cooked meal than the microwave dinners they were going to eat," Joseph said.

"What time do they normally eat?"

"In the summertime, around seven, and in the winter, five. We really only have two seasons on a ranch."

"I'd better get started, then." She went over to the fridge to grab some items. "What time should I have breakfast ready?"

"The guys usually like to come in around nine for breakfast. They've already been up and around a few hours by then and are pretty hungry," he stated.

"That sounds perfect."

"Do you mind if I take Trevor to look at the horses in the barn?" Joseph asked.

"You really don't have to do that, Mr. Anderson. He can hang out in here with me and color," she told him. The last thing she wanted was for her son to be a burden.

"He's no problem, Emily. I enjoy the lad, and no boy wants to hang around the kitchen until the food is all done. Come on, Trevor, you can pick your favorite horse to get acquainted with. The boys love training young ones. We have to let the men know when dinner is ready, anyway," Joseph said. He led Trevor from the room before Emily had a chance to launch a further protest.

She knew Joseph wasn't the type of guy who was told *no* very often. She figured if he got frustrated with her son, he'd bring him back. She started humming to herself as she began several large pots of chicken and dumplings with fresh baked bread.

Chapter Three

Mark slammed his cowboy hat onto the hotel bed and stared at the blinking light on his phone. He'd busted his ass on this business dead, and it had just fallen through. No, it hadn't just fallen through. He'd taken it and rammed it down that worthless SOB's throat.

Metaphorically speaking, of course.

He was normally a happy-go-lucky guy, more likely to crack a joke than ever raise his voice. But today, his mood was poisonous. The guy he'd been speaking to over the last several months had neglected to tell him that the ten thousand head of cattle he was trying to sell were on the brink of death.

One of the few things Mark couldn't tolerate at all was animal abuse. He could understand one guy punching another if legitimately provoked, but a man didn't abuse an animal or ever hurt a woman. Those were pretty basic morals. When he dealt with scum like the guy he'd dealt with that evening, it took everything in him not to revert to his teenage self and whoop the guy one.

He poured himself a stiff drink and let the warmth spread down his throat to help calm his nerves. Only then did he listen to his voice mail.

"Great news, son. I found you a new cook. She's absolutely perfect. She made dinner for the crew tonight, and I think the men gained a few pounds. By the time they had nibbled every last crumb from her apple cobbler, we almost had to have a crane brought in to lift them from the table. Call me back when you get in." His father's voice came across the phone loud and clear.

"Good deal. One less thing I have to worry about," Mark muttered aloud. Pouring himself another drink before he sat down to return his father's call, he took a large sip, knowing he might need it.

"About time you called back," Joseph boomed over the line.

"I'm great, and how are you, Dad?"

"Yeah, yeah… How are you and so on?" Joseph joked back.

His father was working miracles on Mark's mood. In fact, just thinking about the whole crowd, including his sisters-in-law and beautiful nephews and nieces, usually helped keep him chipper and on an even keel. Granted, as the family had grown over the last few years, he'd started to feel a touch of envy as he sat on the sidelines watching the clear love between his brothers and their wives. But he'd never admit that to his father. And right now, he was feeling just fine.

"Did you get the cattle?" Joseph asked.

Correction: *Had been feeling just fine.* "No, the guy turned out to be a real crook," Mark said. Damn. His anger started to boil up again as he told the story to his father.

"Unfortunately, in the business you're in, there are going to be dishonest people. Not everyone is like you, son."

Mark felt warmth spread through his chest at his father's praise. It didn't matter how old he became, he wanted his parents to be pleased with the job he did.

"I know, Dad. It still pains me to see animals mistreated, though. If people aren't going to give this business their all, then they have no business operating a ranch."

"I agree fully. I hope you reported them."

"I did, though all they have to do is claim they couldn't afford the food. It's depressing. Anyway, I don't want to keep you on the phone all night. Besides, I'll see you tomorrow. I'm coming home early, since there's no need to stay here any longer," Mark told him.

"Good. I'll call the rest of the clan, and we can have a big get-together. It's been a few weeks now, which is too long."

"I agree with you. We can have a barbecue at my place. I don't want to overwhelm the new cook, so speak to Mom and Alex and have them bring some food, and I'll give Lucas a ring, and see what he can contribute," Mark said. He was already feeling better at the thought of being with his family.

"I'll do that. I don't see us overwhelming the new cook, though. She's a real peach."

The tone in his father's voice alerted him that something was up. Mark's ears pricked up and he started paying more attention.

"What do you mean, she's a peach?" he asked, then lifted his glass and took a fortifying sip.

"Oh, nothing. She's just a good girl. I liked her instantly," Joseph hedged. His father wasn't a pro at hiding it when he was up to no good. His voice gave him away every single time.

"And how old exactly is this new cook of mine?"

"What does that matter, Mark? As long as the little lady can cook good food, that's all that matters, isn't it?" Joseph huffed.

Mark had to hold back the chuckle at his father's indignant tone. The man didn't like to be caught meddling. He thought he was so dang smooth. Well, Joseph might have been able to fool his brothers, but Mark considered himself a bit smarter than those two, even if they were the ones working in the corporate offices.

"I guess I'll just have to get my information when I get home. I'm warning you, though, if you are trying to set anything up, like I think you did with Lucas and Alex, you are wasting your time. I'm a happy man, and don't need my father messing around in my love life."

The thing was, though, that he wasn't completely satisfied with his life. He'd actually looked around just a bit for some serious companionship. But it was much harder for him to find a woman than people might think. Yes, women were after him constantly, but not for just himself. They wanted the wealth and prestige that came along with the Anderson name.

If Mark ever did marry, it would be for love, the kind of love that his parents shared. He didn't believe in divorce, so when he did walk down the aisle, and he knew it would happen someday, he wanted it to be with a woman he couldn't live without.

He wanted her to feel the exact same way about him.

"I have a long drive back to the city, so I'll talk to you tomorrow," Joseph said, reminding Mark that he was still on the other end of the line.

"Thanks, Dad. See you tomorrow."

Mark hung up the phone and waited a minute before calling his brother. He couldn't help but be a little anxious about what awaited him back home. What had his dad pulled now?

Chapter Four

Side dishes. They wanted side dishes.

"Can you make some side dishes for the family barbecue tonight?" Edward had said to Emily when she came downstairs. "They're bringing everything else."

She was a cook, dammit. Why should side dishes freak her out? Texas Caviar? Grilled blue cheese and bacon potato salad? Cajun deviled eggs? Chili-rubbed vegetable kabobs? Mississippi hush puppies? She could do them while walking in her sleep with both hands tied behind her back.

"Of course," she'd answered.

It wasn't really the side dishes at all. Her boss was going to be home that night, and, worse, bringing his entire family with him. That scared the living bejeebers out of her. What if they didn't like her food? Nah. Couldn't happen. But what if her boss thought she was too young for the job? Possible. And what about Trevor? Did Mark Anderson know that she came with a five-year-old son? Joseph seemed to think everything would be just fine, but the bottom line was that it wasn't his decision. If her boss, this Mark Anderson, didn't want a little boy running around his place while his men were trying to work, she'd have to look for another job right away.

All she could do was make herself so invaluable that he'd look past her youth and the extra mouth to feed. Throwing herself into cooking, she made the crew breakfast and lunch, and then kept at it in the kitchen, working on dishes she hoped would curl the guy's toes.

"Mom, can I please swim now?" Trevor asked as he came running in, wearing his swim trunks and a hopeful expression.

Even at age five, men are such manipulators, she thought with a smile. But she needed a break. "How can I say no to that face? Let me run upstairs and change, and then we can swim for a while. But only if you promise not to complain when it's time to leave the pool. I still have work to do and you can't be in there alone."

"Awww, mom," he whined. She just looked at him sternly. "OK. I promise." He pouted as he sat down to wait for her. It took all of Emily's control not to smile. She couldn't let him know she was amused or he'd try to use that to his advantage.

Trevor was a good boy and she'd spend every minute she had available to make him happy, but it was good for him to realize at a young age that people had to work for hard if they wanted to go places in their lives.

His father had handed him everything just so the boy wouldn't bother him. Not so with her; she wanted Trevor to learn that things he wanted wouldn't just drop into his lap from magic trees.

Right now, she and her son were both getting just what they wanted. The pool would relax her muscles and stressed mind. She played with her son in the shallow end, taking full advantage of the floating toys and enjoying his laughter. They were in the middle of a splashing war when Mark stepped onto the patio.

*****

When Mark caught sight of his new cook, he froze. And then heated up. She was jumping in the air, catching a ball the young boy tossed her, and her wet hair flew upward before slapping against her back. The modest swimsuit hid none of her appealing curves from his view, and to his surprise, he found himself trying to control the tightening of his body.

Standing in the shadows while he tried to figure out — and hide — the desire she'd apparently inspired, he took a moment and watched as she played with a young boy he assumed was her son. His father hadn't mentioned that the new cook had an extra person in tow. He'd also been very sly not to mention her age or beauty. Her laughter carried over, making Mark want to strip down to his swim trunks — definitely not Speedos — and join them.

She climbed from the pool, the water dripping from her flawless body. Her long dark hair cascaded down her back, drawing his eyes to the sweet swell of her hips. Yet though she had curves in all the right places, he was still mystified by the instant attraction.

Yes, he'd been drawn to many women before, but he couldn't remember the last time just the sight of a female had his heart pounding, and his body hardening. Maybe it had been too long since his last date. When he realized he couldn't remember when he'd last gone out, he knew it had been too long. So that was the reason…

The woman finally looked up, and her stunning dark eyes fastened on him. They rounded in surprise and she gazed at him for what felt like hours. After a few moments, she seemed to pull herself from their mutual trance, wrapped a towel around herself, and began walking toward him.

Mark forced himself to adopt a relaxed posture as he waited. She was just his new cook. So what if she was hotter than hell? All he cared about was the food she prepared. *Yeah, right!*

*****

Emily took a deep breath and introduced herself. "Hi, I'm Emily, and you must be my boss," she said with a bright smile. She had no doubt the man standing before her was Mark Anderson; his air and demeanor shouted *man in charge.* She was hoping that if she faked her confidence well enough, he would see past the fact she had a son and allow her to keep her job.

Here's what was really unjust: that he was one of the most attractive men she'd even laid eyes upon. She hadn't been counting on that — not at all. He was well over six feet tall and solidly built with muscles in all the right places, and a tight shirt and fitted jeans hiding nothing from her view. His dark hair was covered by a worn Stetson, and his sea-blue eyes seemed as if they didn't miss a thing. She was having a hard time looking away from those mesmerizing eyes.

He looked her up and down before finally replying. "Mark Anderson. You're the new cook my father hired?" he asked, though it was fairly obvious, as she was the only adult stranger on his property.

"Yes, I'm Emily Jackson..."

Trevor had noticed the new man and came running up the steps of the pool. In his eagerness, he interrupted his mother. "Hi, I'm Trevor. I like your hat."

"Trevor, honey, back up a little! You're dripping water all over Mr. Anderson's boots," she said, gasping in horror. She was trying to tread lightly, and there Trevor was, drowning the poor man's hand-tooled leather.

Mark bent down so he was eye level with Trevor. "It's OK, little man. You can call me Mark. Are you enjoying the pool?" he asked.

"It's the biggest and best pool ever, and the puppies are so cute, and did you know there are horses everywhere and Doug said he's going to teach me how to ride them and everything," Trevor said all in one breath.

Mark laughed at Trevor's enthusiasm and then ruffled his hair. Emily finally allowed herself to relax. Not only was the man drop-dead gorgeous, but he also had a soft spot for kids. She didn't know men like him existed anymore. So it was possible he wasn't going to fire her right there and then.

"Maybe you can help me pick which one of the puppies we keep and give it a name," Mark said. That sealed it. He wouldn't let Trevor name a puppy only to send her and Trevor away. No one did that.

Trevor's face fell instantly, with tears welling in his eyes. "What's wrong, baby?" Emily asked as she dropped to her knees next to Mark.

"Why do the puppies have to leave?" he asked Mark as the tears began spilling down his face.

Mark looked completely taken aback. It was obvious the man didn't know how to handle the tears of children. She had no idea that when his niece Jasmine cried, he just gave her whatever she wanted. Emily got ready to explain to Trevor that the puppies would be going to good homes, but Mark spoke before she could.

"We'll keep all the puppies. There's plenty of room for them to run around here. You can name them all," Mark said.

Emily didn't know what to say, and was trying to find a way to tell her new boss that he didn't need to promise such a thing to her son, that Trevor would get over the heartache of seeing the puppies leave.

"You promise?" Trevor asked with skepticism.

"Scout's honor."

"Thank you!" Trevor squealed. His tears instantly evaporated, and he launched himself into Mark's arms. Mark held him close and Emily was fighting her own tears as her son soaked Mark's clothes without the man appearing to notice.

"Trevor, you shouldn't ask Mr. Anderson to do such a thing. What about all the other kids who would like to have a puppy?" she asked.

"But, Mom, there are lots of puppies out there that they can have, and I've never had a doggy before," he whined.

"It really is OK, Emily, I promise. I like to have lots of dogs here. They protect the cattle," Mark said. She looked into the pleading faces of both her young son and her new boss and knew that she'd been beaten. It was Mark's ranch, after all. If he wanted to keep the dogs, then that was his decision.

"Of course, Mr. Anderson," she said with a tight smile. Trevor beamed and put his arms back around Mark's neck.

Emily had to turn away for a moment at the way her son clutched the man close. Trevor's father had bought the child everything under the sun, but he'd never just stopped and hugged him, given him the affection he needed and deserved.

She could see herself developing a crush on her boss, and there was no way she would allow that to happen. She needed the job, and men like Mark didn't settle down with women like her. Only two things could happen between them — red-hot sex and then a cold pink slip, or fired up, then fired. She almost wished he were a buttoned-up bully instead of a sexy cowboy with a soft heart for children.

"Trevor, let's head inside. I need to finish getting dinner prepared, so I can't watch you out here anymore," she said, turning toward the house.

"Ah, Mom, I want to swim some more, please?" he begged.

"I'll bring you out to swim tomorrow, but I really need to finish dinner. Remember what we talked about earlier," she said.

"OK," he said dejectedly as he finally let go of Mark.

"I was planning on taking a swim. I'll keep an eye on him," Mark said. "Hang with your mom in the kitchen for a few minutes while I run upstairs to change clothes," he told Trevor, and then jogged into the house, not waiting for a reply from Emily.

So Mark was just like his father — not used to being told no. Emily wasn't about to argue with him. But she did have a talk with Trevor. If the boy wasn't on his best behavior, she'd…well, she'd figure something out.

Mark quickly collected Trevor, and she heard them splashing in the pool.

She enjoyed herself in the kitchen, preparing food while listening to the sound of her son's laughter through the open door. Before she knew it, everything was ready.

She checked on Trevor, who was more than content to be splashing around with Mark, so allowed herself a luxurious bubble bath. She laid her head back against the tub and sighed out loud. She couldn't believe how lucky she was to have found such a great job and a good boss.

If she'd been a pessimistic sort of person, she'd have been waiting for the other shoe to drop.

Chapter Five

Emily could tell she needed a new dictionary. *Family barbecue, noun: In Anderson terms, a massive indoor and outdoor blowout featuring more than a hundred beautiful people, a mountain of both ribs and ribbing, and more thrills, chills and shrill children than you can shake a stick at.*

Everyone was smiling, and laughter could be heard above the sound of the country music playing in the background.

The grills were lit, and the sweet smell of good meat being barbecued made her mouth water and her stomach growl a little tune. She'd been so busy preparing food all day that she'd forgotten to eat anything. She hadn't been sure whether she should join the party, but Edward had told her that staff was always invited.

"You must be Emily, the new cook, no?" asked an attractive dark-haired man. Emily had been observing all the people around her and hadn't noticed the couple approach her. They could have both graced the cover of *GQ*, and she was a bit intimidated.

"Yes, I am," she finally managed to reply.

"It's great to meet you, Emily. I'm Amy, and this obnoxious man here is Lucas, Mark's older brother," she said pleasantly.

"It's really nice to meet you," Emily replied shyly.

"Don't let this crowd overwhelm you too much; they are all great people. My first time around them nearly scared me to death, and now I can't imagine how miserable my life would be without every member of this family," she said. As Amy was talking, she looked up at her husband and gave him a tender look of love.

Emily wasn't sure whether they were done talking and she should walk away and leave them alone.

"Oh, would you guys quit with the gazing thing? You're obviously making poor Emily here uncomfortable," another extremely gorgeous guy broke in, saving Emily from her dilemma.

"Whatever, Alex; you know you have trouble being ten feet away from poor Jessica without keeling over from want of…*stimulation*," Lucas teased his brother.

"Well, when you're right, I guess you're right," Alex said. "Hi, I'm the middle brother, Alex, and my beautiful wife is getting the kids settled but will be over in a few minutes. I have to tell you, Emily, you're far hotter than the last cook," he added with a wink.

Emily could feel her face turn a deep shade of red; she hated that her emotions were so easy to read. Since she didn't know how to reply to Alex's comment, she decided to not say anything.

"You boys just never grow up now, do you?"

Emily turned toward the voice, which belonged to another attractive woman, who was wrapping her arm in Alex's.

"Never mind them," the woman said with a glint in her eyes. "They love to get a reaction out of a pretty lady. When they met poor Amy for the first time, she got proposed to by all three brothers. By the way, I'm Jessica, and obviously married to this rogue here." She indicated Alex. "They're all talk and no action, though."

"Oh, really? I take that as a challenge," Alex said and then proceeded to dip Jessica low to the ground. She let out a girlish giggle, but then his lips met hers and it became obvious she'd forgotten anyone else was around.

"Um…you two want to go on upstairs, or do you want to continue to embarrass my new cook?" Mark asked while strolling up to the growing group.

Alex slowly lifted his head, only to glare at Mark. "I would much prefer to kick the crap out of you, but that can wait until later," he finally said and punched his brother in the arm. To Emily, the punch looked hard enough to knock a normal man to the ground, but Mark just laughed and asked his brother if that was all he had.

"You boys go help with the grilling. We're going to sneak some dessert," Amy said and then put one arm through Emily's and the other through Jessica's and dragged them off to the dessert table.

Emily had to hold back tears. She was overwhelmed at being included so easily with the obviously loving family. She'd never really had girlfriends before and hoped she would be around long enough to become friends with the two women, as they seemed like people she would definitely want to know.

"Tell all. What was your reaction to seeing Mark for the first time?" Amy asked as she stopped at a table groaning under the number of pies, cakes, cookies and other delights that covered it.

"I…uh…" Emily didn't know what to say. Mark was her boss and she didn't want to tell his sisters-in-law that she'd been drooling over him more than she was drooling now over the sweets in front of them.

"It's OK. The first time I laid eyes on the three men standing together in a room, I had to keep the drool inside my mouth. They are all delicious. My heart belongs to Lucas, of course, but the men are certainly pieces of…art."

"Yes, they really are," Emily admitted with a small chuckle.

"Imagine growing up around them. I was such a wallflower and had the biggest crush on Alex, but he didn't know I was alive until a night we were playing tag and ended up on the ground together. That was my first kiss," Jessica said with a remembered sigh.

"Oh, I can't imagine you being a wallflower," Emily said with shock as she looked at the stunning woman before her.

"I've become much more secure and confident. Having the love of a good man will do that to a woman. I am head over heels in love with my husband, though there were times in the beginning of our marriage that I really thought I'd end up knocking him out cold," Jessica admitted.

"Ditto. Lucas was a royal pain in the arse for a while. But I've trained him well. He's really just a gentle giant," Amy said as she picked up a beautifully decorated cupcake and took a bite, sighing in bliss.

"Well, I am just the new cook," Emily said, wanting to make sure these women knew she didn't have designs on the youngest brother.

The two women giggled. "You may want to tell Mark that. He's been following you with his eyes since we walked away. Make sure you add an extra wiggle to your hips to really make him pant," Amy said, making Emily blush again.

"Oh, we're being terrible. What you must think of us," Jessica said as she loaded up her plate, then waited while Emily selected some treats.

"You are both fine. I just don't want people to think I'm chasing the boss. You know how those clichés go," Emily said as she took a bite from a gooey brownie. "This is amazing."

"Oh, those are from a bakery I'll have to show you. They make the best goodies ever."

"I have a difficult time buying from bakeries. I love to make things from scratch," Emily admitted, though she wouldn't mind talking to the baker there and seeing whether she could trade a few recipes.

"It's OK to cheat once in a while. Just wait till you see the amount of food these cowboys consume. It's insane," Jessica said.

The three women moved toward a table with their ill-gotten goodies and continued visiting. Emily relaxed, almost. She did keep her eye out for Trevor. He was playing with all the newly arrived children and clearly in heaven.

Heaven. Yes. This was pure heaven, she thought.

Chapter Six

Mark couldn't take his eyes off of Emily as she walked away. The way her hips were swaying in her short summer dress was enough to lock his attention onto her for the foreseeable future. Hell, it was probably enough to get him locked up — he could picture his hands sneaking up her skirt to discover what she was wearing underneath the floral print.

As he stood there, a wisp of wind picked up the hem of the dress, showing him more of her incredible shapely thighs. He held his breath as he wished for a larger gust to take the dress up a little bit higher. His pants became too tight again, making him grimace. And caught up as he was in his thoughts and feelings, he missed the look that passed between his two brothers. If he had seen it, maybe he'd have been more prepared for what followed.

"Your new cook is sure hot," Lucas said casually.

"Yeah, if I were single, I would hire her in a heartbeat, whether she could cook or not," Alex added.

"I haven't really noticed," Mark said.

"So you aren't interested in her?" Lucas questioned.

"Of course I'm not. She's an employee, and I prefer to keep it professional," he said. Was he trying to lie to them or to himself? Immaterial. He wasn't a randy teenager anymore, and he could control himself.

"Well, in that case, I saw Don over there eyeing her. I think I'll try some matchmaking," Lucas said slyly.

"Like hell you will," Mark exclaimed. He then seemed to pull himself together a bit and added, "I don't want employees to be having romances, because when things go bad, it makes life around them miserable, and one or both of them will quit. I'd have to do the whole hiring thing over again." He felt he'd made a pretty good save from his little outburst.

"I do see your point, Mark. Hey! I know this great guy at the office," Alex said and winked at Lucas. "Just the other day, he was asking me if I knew any single women. I think he and Emily would make a good match, and he doesn't work here at the ranch."

Both brothers could practically see steam rising out of Mark's ears. It wouldn't have come as a surprise to anyone who knew them that they were enjoying themselves immensely at their brother's expense.

"Would you please leave my cook alone?" Mark almost yelled. Several heads turned toward the brothers. None of them saw the grin on the face of one particular witness — Joseph, who was within hearing distance.

"So, Joseph, it looks like your matchmaking is working once again, you sly old man," said Edward, who was standing next to him.

"Why, Edward, I have no idea what you're talking about," Joseph replied.

"You forget how well I know you, sir. Before I came here, I worked for you for too many years not to know when you're up to something. Besides, since when does the cook have the bedroom right next door to Mark's?"

"Well, talk a little quieter. If that boy learns I'm trying to pair him up, he'll take off running in the opposite direction. Even worse, if Katherine hears about it, I'll never hear the end of it," Joseph said, looking around guiltily.

"If you weren't so busy meddling, you wouldn't have anything to be worried about," Edward said. "I do have to commend you on your taste, however. Emily's a breath of fresh air, and little Trevor is full of energy. It's nice to see a pretty lady and a young lad in the house."

Joseph puffed up his chest from the praise. He *did* have great taste, if he said so himself, and he looked over at Amy and Jessica as if to prove his point. He'd done the matchmaking with his first two boys, and look how well that had turned out.

"Grampa, Grampa, I have a new friend," came the insistent voice of his eldest granddaughter, Jasmine. She was pulling on his pant leg, trying to get his undivided attention.

"I can see that. Are you playing nicely?" he asked his mischievous granddaughter.

"I love him, Grampa. We're going to get married," she declared in utmost seriousness.

Joseph had to laugh at the look on Trevor's face. Even when he was only five years old, the word *marriage* scared a male.

"Why don't you gather your cousins? We'll have some dinner, and afterward we can make s'mores." he suggested.

Jasmine was instantly diverted and grabbed Trevor's hand, then raced off to find her siblings and cousins.

Trevor was fitting in nicely with the grandchildren, just as Joseph knew he would. He was a good lad and Joseph wouldn't have minded at all having another grandson. The more, the merrier.

"What are you boys up to over here looking all sly?"

Joseph turned guilty eyes toward his wife. She could see right through him, so his best option was to use evasive tactics.

"You look so stunning tonight, dear. Have I told you that yet?"

Even after almost half a century together, he could still make his bride blush, and it filled him with wonder.

"You are a devil, Joseph Anderson, but your strategy has worked. I'll leave you to your meddling. Just know that I have my eye on you," she said as she leaned against him and pressed her lips to his.

"Ah, Katherine, you make my heart full," he told her — truthfully. She caressed his cheek before she turned to go and join her daughters-in-law.

"I understand your desire for your sons to have happy marriages. You have been blessed time and again with your beautiful wife, Joseph," Edward told him as the two men watched Katherine's graceful movements across the well-manicured lawn.

"Yes, I have, dear friend, yes, I have," Joseph said with a sigh.

He had a growing family and was in the best of health. If only his brother had been here, he'd have felt complete. It had been a while since he'd been able to get ahold of George. In fact, if he didn't hear from him soon, he was going to send out a search party.

His brother had lost his wife four years ago, and Joseph knew that had to be beyond devastating. Joseph couldn't imagine how he would go on without his Katherine, but he knew one thing for sure, and that was that he'd need his family more than ever if something that terrible were to happen.

George needed to be with Joseph or he'd never get over his loss. It was time that Joseph gave his twin some tough love and dragged him to Seattle if he had to. Enough time had passed, and their family needed to be together as one.

Pushing those thoughts aside for now, Joseph focused back on the family in front of him. He was a blessed man, indeed.

Chapter Seven

"Water volleyball? Are you crazy? Everyone will sink straight to the bottom of the pool," Emily exclaimed.

She'd looked at the plundered tables with awe. Only a couple of hours earlier she'd never have believed that all the food that had filled the space could possibly be eaten, but she hadn't counted on hardworking ranchers and growing kids. She'd made enough food to feed a small country, and on top of that, everyone who'd attended had brought at least one dish, and it was all gone. Only a few scraps and crumbs were left lying around, doubtless for lucky dogs.

"C'mon, Emily," Jessica said. "We need another person; come change with us and play. We need to work off some of those calories, and you should help us out because your great cooking is in large part to blame."

Emily was uncomfortable prancing around in her swimsuit in front of a bunch of strangers, and she might have used her son as an excuse, but no such luck. Trevor was in the house with the rest of the kids, listening to Joseph read stories. After story time, the youngsters were all going to camp out in the huge den and watch movies. Jessica's nanny, Julia, had offered to stay with them in case any of them woke and needed something. And after knowing Trevor for only a few hours, the Anderson family members were all treating her son as if he were one of their own. In short, the old "sorry, my kid needs me" gambit wouldn't wash.

The volleyball did sound like fun, and she didn't want to disappoint Jessica, so Emily decided to get over her fears.

They quickly changed and ran back down the stairs. The men were already in the water, hitting the ball back and forth and dunking each other in the process. Mark jumped out of the water to spike the ball over the net and Emily forgot to breathe for a few moments.

Tall, dark, handsome, and succulently wet. The water cascading down his muscled chest and arms glistened on the deep tan he'd acquired from working long and hard outside. Heck, that work was clearly better than any gym. Mark's hair was a little on the long side, and she found herself wanting to run her fingers through the wet strands. The waistband of his swim trunks was riding low, showing her the trail of hair that led past his navel. She noticed where her eyes had strayed and instantly yanked her head away, praying no one else had been watching the way she'd reacted to her boss.

"Hey, you guys aren't allowed to start without us," Amy scolded the boys. She ran over and jumped off the side of the pool, making a huge splash with a perfectly executed cannonball.

"That's called cheating when you try to blind your opponent," Lucas said before grabbing her up in a searing kiss. Emily could swear she saw steam rising up off the water.

"Hey, I don't mind scratching this whole game and heading in if you guys are too busy to play," Alex said to Lucas and Amy before he turned and leered at his curvy wife in her fitted bikini.

"No chance," Jessica replied. She then grabbed Emily's hand and pulled her into the pool with her.

Emily came to the surface coughing up water. Suddenly, there was a hand pounding on her back. "Are you okay?" Mark asked, standing too close to her hormone-addled body. The feel of his hand on her bare skin was sending her senses into overdrive.

"I'm fine. I just wasn't expecting that and forgot to plug my nose," she coughed out.

"I'm so sorry, Emily." Jessica said.

"I'm fine; I promise. Let's play," Emily said. She disliked being the center of attention in any setting, let alone when she was in a bikini in front of a very virile man—scratch that — in front of several virile men.

Some of the ranch hands and their girlfriends were playing against the Anderson siblings and their spouses in a couple palooza, and Emily cringed to realize that she was Mark's partner. She hoped he didn't think she had engineered the pairing.

But Emily soon lost herself in the game. The brothers, though competitive, were a blast to be with. They were constantly cracking jokes or laughing about something, at least when they weren't sneaking in kisses with their wives.

The ball came directly toward Emily, and she made a dive to save it before it hit the water. Not looking where she was going, she suddenly slammed into the rock-solid chest of Mark, and his arms automatically encircled her to keep her from falling into the water again and having another choking fit. She looked up, and their eyes locked on to each other.

She couldn't pull away from him, no matter how much her brain was telling her to laugh and thank him and then let go. He had the most spellbinding blue eyes she'd ever seen. She automatically leaned into him, forgetting that anyone else was near them or that they were in the middle of a game.

Mark closed the gap and hungrily took her lips, pulling her tightly against his wet chest. His arms wrapped around her bare waist, and he pulled her against the solid mass poking into her stomach. "*Oh, this is a good kiss*" was all that went through her brain.

Suddenly, a splash came over the top of both their heads, making Emily choke again. Mark jerked back, about to kill whoever was guilty of the interruption, when he noticed all eyes around the pool were on the two of them. He looked back at Emily's face and saw the dawning horror in her eyes.

He could practically read her thoughts. He'd barely met the woman, but her face was an open book for anyone who wanted to read it. Her already flushed cheeks had turned a becoming shade of red, and she scooted back from him, as if he had the plague.

Mark was trying to figure out what he could possibly say to make the situation better when his brother decided to help him. "Geez, Mark, can you quit manhandling the poor girl? I know the water is a bit chilly, but there are other ways to warm up, like actually playing the game."

"Look who's talking," Mark spouted back, and then all the men started a water fight. The women ran for cover and climbed from the pool.

Thoroughly mortified, Emily was trying to think of the best way to escape without being obvious about it. She couldn't believe she'd behaved like that, especially in front of an audience. She was the cook, not Mark's girlfriend.

"Seriously, I know you're a bit embarrassed by the kiss, but these guys aren't easy to resist. Just know each of us has been there, and no one's thinking anything, except, maybe, *That's one lucky girl,*" Amy said.

Emily gave her a crooked smile of thanks and decided Amy might be right and probably no one had paid much attention. Besides, they'd been in the water and pretty much covered up. She wrapped a towel tightly around herself and decided to forget about the whole thing.

"I thought you said you weren't interested," Alex teased Mark.

"I didn't mean for that to happen. Hell, I don't know what happened," Mark said, a little dazedly.

"I guess you would take exception if I set her up, then?" Alex added.

Mark just scowled at him before swimming away. Lucas and Alex looked at each other with an understanding smile. They were both familiar with the pain their brother was going through. They'd fought their attraction to their wives, and, looking back, they realized what utter idiots they had been.

Everyone got changed into dry clothes, and most of the guests started heading out. Mark stoked the fire in the backyard pit, and the family sat together, telling stories until the early hours of the morning. Emily tried to excuse herself to let the family have time together, but Jessica and Amy had decided she was their new best friend and insisted she stay.

She didn't fight them very hard. She was having a delightful time herself and didn't want to go up to her room all alone.

"I need to get some sleep," Lucas finally said and then waggled his eyebrows at Amy. Emily could feel the slight blush returning to her face at witnessing the man's clear intent. Jessica and Alex soon followed them, and suddenly, Emily found herself alone with Mark.

The fire had died down to little more than embers, and it was barely light enough to see his shadowed face. "I'd better get some sleep, myself," she said and forced out a yawn. What a joke. She was so wound up, she'd need an Australian sheep ranch to count before she got any sleep.

Mark placed his hand on her arm when she tried to get up. She sat motionless, not knowing what to say or do. If he wanted to speak to her, she was obligated to listen.

"Emily, I'm really sorry about what happened in the pool. Seriously, I don't usually grab women and make out with them in front of my whole family," he said, absentmindedly mussing his hair.

She was itching to smooth his hair back into place, but she managed to tuck both hands beneath her thighs. "It's no problem. I wasn't an unwilling participant, but I'm sorry, too. Honestly, I don't usually do that either," she said.

"OK, we're both sorry," he said and then smiled.

The man should be registered as a lethal weapon so women could be forewarned, Emily thought.

"So we're friends, right?" he asked.

"Yes, of course," she replied, finally feeling the pressure in her chest start to ease.

"Good," he said. "Want to see something really cool?"

"Sure."

He grabbed her hand and started leading her toward the barn. She assumed he would let go, but he kept holding on and she didn't have the willpower to pull away. He was part of a very touchy-feely family; that was it, nothing more.

"My favorite mare is about to give birth. There's nothing more miraculous and beautiful than that," he told her excitedly.

Emily found herself eager to see the new foal. They got to the barn and heard some pained noises. Emily looked up in concern. "Is she OK?"

"She's fine. I've been checking on her the past couple of days, and the vet has been watching over her. Everything is on schedule, and the foal is in the right position. Giving birth still hurts, though."

"Yes, it *does*!" she agreed.

"I guess you would know more than I would," he said with a sheepish shrug.

Emily laughed and then quieted as they approached the stall with the laboring horse. She was beautiful, with a shining dark brown coat and a bulging belly.

"How you doing, girl?" Mark spoke softly to the mare.

The animal seemed to roll her eyes at the clueless man, or that's what Emily liked to believe. She remembered when she was giving birth and the doctors had asked how she was doing. She'd wanted to punch them as hard as she could and then ask them the same thing. Guys had no idea.

"You're a pretty girl," Emily said in a soft, low voice while gently rubbing the animal's nose. The mare whinnied at her as if to say, A*t least you understand,* and then went back to ignoring them both.

Emily didn't know how much time they spent there, but as the sky started to lighten, the mare finally pushed the new foal out, with some help from Mark. Emily looked at her boss sitting on the floor with the gangly baby in his lap, and felt her heart pounding. He was covered in dirt and blood and still irresistible.

Once the whole ordeal was over, she realized how exhausted she was. The sun was coming over the hill, and she figured she'd better try to get a few hours of sleep.

"Thanks for sharing this with me. It really was amazing," she whispered, not wanting to startle the new horse.

"Thanks for keeping me company. I didn't mean to keep you up all night."

"It was well worth it," she responded.

Since Mark was busy making sure the new horse was healthy, Emily slipped from the barn and headed back to the house. She lay down, and her last thoughts before finally succumbing to exhaustion were about her new employer.

Keeping her distance would be a problem.

Chapter Eight

Emily jerked upright in bed and frantically tried to wipe the sleep from her eyes. One o'clock in the afternoon. What if her son had grown scared when he woke up and his mom wasn't there?

She took a two-minute shower, dressed, and scurried down the stairs. She came running around the corner into the dining room, and stopped. Trevor was sitting there happily with all the other kids, Mark, and his siblings. None of the adults looked as if they had been up very long.

"Mom, did you know a baby horse was born this morning, and as soon as we're done eating lunch, Mark is going to take me down to see her?" he practically squealed.

"I did know. I got to watch her being born. I'm so sorry, darling, that I wasn't awake with you this morning."

"It's OK, Mom, I didn't know you weren't awake. We've been playing all day long," Trevor told her.

Emily felt a stab of disappointment that her child didn't need her as much as he used to. She covered her distress by going over to the table and grabbing some sandwich fixings. OK, here was something to feel guilty about.

"I'm sorry I didn't make you breakfast," she said to the room in general.

"You can't work seven days a week, Emily. I think Edward already told you that on the weekends everyone fends for themselves," Mark said before stuffing his mouth. He was acting as if he were at his last meal.

"I know that's the case normally, but with your family here, they probably would have enjoyed a nice breakfast," she argued. No one was letting her play the female martyr, dammit.

"If the rest of your food is anything like some of those salads and dishes you made last night, we most certainly would have enjoyed your breakfast. But it's nice to have a make-your-own-sandwich lunch, plus I found a couple of bowls of your salad that somehow didn't make it out to the food table last night," Amy said, looking pointedly at Mark.

"Hey, I love potato salad, and I wanted some saved for today," Mark said.

Emily knew she'd brought that bowl out, so Mark must have sneaked it back in. But here at last was gratification, fulfillment of her womanly destiny, she joked silently. He was piling *her food* into his mouth.

"Seriously, I snuck into some early last night and then had to spirit it away. I haven't had homemade salad this good since… Well, hell, since never. No offense to Mom," he added.

"You do know the way to a man's heart is through his stomach…among other things," Alex said with a wink.

"Amen," Mark added, without even pausing in his chewing.

Emily must be getting used to his family, because she was blushing far less already. She knew the brothers were just ribbing each other, and they didn't mean any harm. She simply had to get used to the way they talked to one another if she wanted to be comfortable around them.

After everyone ate, the adults gathered up the younger kids while the older ones clung to Mark as he led them all to the barn. Emily was amazed when she saw the newborn foal up and wobbling around in the open space of the barn.

"She was just born; I can't believe she's already walking," she gasped.

The three brothers laughed. "Newborn animals are much more independent than human babies," Lucas said.

"Hey, speak for yourself. I've always been one of a kind and able to do things faster than the average person," Mark said.

"I don't think so; we all know I've always been the smartest one," Alex said as he thumped his chest.

"You're all abnormally strong, sexy, and very, very smart," Jessica said.

"You're all those things and so much more," Alex said before kissing her.

"OK, I simply haven't gotten enough sleep to deal with the two of you playing kissy face," Mark grumbled.

"Considering I found you down here asleep on the hay, you get a little bit of leeway for grumpiness," Alex conceded. "Of course, a *romp* in the hay would have put you in a much better mood," he added with a wink at Emily.

She pretended to not hear that last statement or notice the wink. "Isn't the baby horse sweet?" she asked Trevor.

"Mom, horses aren't sweet; they're cool," he grumbled.

"Oh, sorry about that," she said with a twinkle in her eye. She loved the way her son was growing up so quickly. Some days, it broke her heart to think he would be a man before she knew it, but at the same time, he had so much personality and such a great heart. She wanted to keep him close to her forever.

"She's a great-looking girl," Lucas said.

"Agreed, brother; another fine addition to the ranch," Alex chimed in.

"Thanks, guys," Mark said.

"We have to get going but can come back next weekend," Lucas said.

"Ah, Dad, I want to play with Trevor some more," Jasmine cried.

"I promise we'll come back for you to play with Trevor, but Mom has an appointment she can't miss, honey," Lucas said sadly. Because he hated to see her upset about anything, he was a pushover with his daughter. The businessmen he'd dealt with through the years would have been flabbergasted to see how easily his daughter was able to get her way with him.

"OK, Daddy," she said in a wobbly voice. She then threw her arms around Trevor. "I will miss you so much," she sniffled.

Lucas was about to tell her they could stay a while longer when Amy gave him her "mother" look. His wife was the only other person able to get away with anything, and he sure as hell wasn't going to argue with her. The repercussions might have been…er…painful — not that he'd ever been stupid enough to find out.

Trevor hugged Jasmine back before noticing what he was doing. "See ya soon," he mumbled. Emily could tell he was trying to be tough in front of Mark, but the boy was close to tears himself.

"Hey, little guy, after all these other kids get out of here, you and I can take a horseback ride up the trails," Mark said as he ruffled Trevor's hair.

"Really?" Trevor's sadness instantly evaporated as he looked hopefully up at Mark.

"Really," Mark stated. "We can even invite your mom if she'd like to come," he added.

Trevor looked over at his mother, as if he was really thinking about it, before finally saying, "I guess she could come with us. She does make good picnic stuff."

"Thanks," Emily said. "I know that was such a hard decision for you," she added with a smile.

"We have to take off, too; see you soon. Let's have a spa day," Jessica said before grabbing Emily in a hug.

"That sounds wonderful," Emily replied, even though she didn't know how long it would take for her to be able to afford that. If Jessica invited her too soon, she would have to make up some excuse to put it off.

After everyone else left, Emily, her son and her boss set off for their ride. She'd never ridden before, so she was given an older mare that was tame and easy to handle, and she felt almost liberated. Trevor sat on the horse with Mark and looked adorable in his arms. She was going to have to fight her attraction to the man with every ounce of willpower she had.

The day ended about as perfectly as it had begun. Mark was witty and charming and had unending patience with her son. Too witty, too charming, and too patient. She told herself repeatedly that they would be at most just friends, and she figured if she lied to herself enough, she'd start to believe it.

Maybe it would be best if she dated so she wouldn't be tempted to fall into Mark's arms. That was probably the safest route to go. Not that Mark was necessarily "into" her, but she could see danger signs flashing all over the place.

As she lay in bed that night, she decided she'd best come up with a plan fast before she did something foolish and jeopardized her job. That would be tragic for both her and Trevor. They'd already been through so much.

Chapter Nine

Problem solved. In the two weeks following the "family" barbecue, Emily had managed to keep everything professional with Mark — whew! — and she was even attracted to the new guy he'd hired on, Chris. Not nearly as attracted to him as she was to Mark, but that was a completely different issue, and she refused to go there. She wouldn't fall for him, there was no future in it, so she needed to be attracted to other men. Case closed.

"Oh, excuse me." Emily had run smack into a gentleman who was looking lost as he held up a fresh peach.

"It was my fault," he automatically replied with a sheepish smile.

Emily laughed, as she was the one clearly in the wrong. Maybe a little bit less daydreaming and a whole lot more paying attention to where she was going were in order.

"Do you need some help with that fruit?" This was something Emily was used to. Most men hadn't the foggiest idea how to pick out fresh fruit or vegetables. It was a skill that took time to learn.

"Would you mind?" he asked, relief written all over his face.

"Not at all. When you select a peach, smell it first," she said, lifting one up and bringing it to her nose, enjoying the fragrance. "Look for — OK, smell for — a pleasingly sweet fragrance. They're related to roses, you know."

She wasn't paying attention to the man's reaction, but her small demonstration had clearly impressed him.

"See, this one smells divine," she said as she offered the piece of fruit to him.

"Yes, it does," he murmured as he held the fruit.

"Next, you look for a creamy gold to yellow undercolor. Despite rumors to the contrary, no, the blush of a peach doesn't indicate ripeness. OK?"

"Yeah! Great."

"Now gently feel the fruit. It should be soft, but not mushy. Mushiness means it's overripe. Also, be careful because they bruise easily, so don't squeeze too hard. Now, see if you can select a few ripe ones."

The man picked one up, smelled it, then put it back. On the third try, he smiled triumphantly as he held it out to her as if it were a gold trophy.

"Perfect. See, you're a natural," she said, patting his arm and making a soft pink suffuse his cheeks.

"I really appreciate your help," he said, holding out his hand. "My name's Joshua."

"Hi, Joshua; I'm Emily. It was really nice to meet you. I'm new in town," she told him.

"Really? That's why I haven't seen you before. Did you move here for work?"

"Yes, I'm cooking for Mark Anderson. It's a wonderful job. I really should be going, though. I have to get these groceries back to the ranch."

"I understand. I do appreciate your help; I'll have to pay you back for the favor sometime," he said with a friendly smile.

"That sounds perfect. I'll see you around," she said before turning and grabbing the last of her produce before she made her way to the register.

One thing that Emily loved so much about living in such a small town was how friendly all the people seemed to be. She'd yet run into anyone who was rude or unhelpful. It was so very different from her experiences in L.A.

"Hi, Emily, let me give you a hand."

Emily turned to find Chris running up to assist her with the groceries.

"What are you doing away from the ranch? I figured you'd be knee deep in the mud right about now," she said as she lifted her trunk and Chris began loading the bags inside.

"I had to pick up some supplies," he said as he finished and leaned on her trunk. "Do you have any other stops to make?"

"Nope, this was my last one. I think I may sneak over to the café, though, and grab a bite to eat. You know what they say about cooks hating to eat their own food."

"Well, I have about an hour to waste while I wait on a part, so if you don't mind, I'll join you," he said. "Then it wouldn't be wasted."

Emily felt a slight blush steal across her cheeks. It was an innocent suggestion, but still, it was sort of like a date. This was what she wanted, right? Of course it was.

"I'd love to have the company," she said, trying her best at flirting, not that she was any good at it. At least he didn't call her on her pathetic attempt.

"Perfect. I'll even buy," he said with a wink.

Her slight blush flared and she quickly looked down at the ground.

Chris took her arm and wrapped it through his as they left her car and moved down the sidewalk toward the café only a block away.

"How do you like working for Mark?" he asked.

"He's a wonderful boss. Plus, he treats Trevor so well that I can have no complaints," she said.

"Yeah, he's a decent boss," he said, but something about his tone alerted her that all might not be paradise in Chris's opinion.

"Is something wrong?" she asked him. She couldn't imagine what.

"Oh, sorry, no, nothing at all. I just haven't worked a ranch in a long time. My body is more sore than I care to admit," he answered with a laugh, and her muscles eased.

She wanted to like this man, but she wouldn't if he badmouthed Mark. It wasn't because she had a crush on Mark — she didn't, she tried to convince herself. She just didn't like it when people slammed others behind their backs. That had been the sort of thing her former in-laws did.

"What did you do before working for Mark?" Emily said.

They had arrived at the café and easily found a table since it was past the usual lunch rush.

"Oh, I've done it all," he said.

"Ah, yes. I've worked my share of jobs, too. My favorites have always included cooking, though. I enjoyed it from the time I was a little girl. I had wonderful parents; they were amazing, in fact, but they passed in a car accident three years ago. I still miss them more than anything," she said with a sigh.

"Are you from here?"

"No. I moved up from California." She really didn't want to get into that.

"What made you move all the way up here? Depending on where you were in California, this is a pretty drastic weather change," he said, smiling easily at her.

"It's a long, boring story," she said evasively.

"We have time," he offered. "That is if you ever need to talk. I won't push it, though," he added when he saw her shoulders tense.

"I appreciate it, Chris. I'd rather leave the past behind me." She was done with her old life, and she wanted only to move forward.

The waitress came and they placed their order, and then chatted about life on a ranch. By the time they left, Emily was thinking she wouldn't mind a real date with Chris. He was a nice guy, easy to talk to, and intelligent.

Still, he wasn't Mark.

Chapter Ten

One day started to run into the next. Mark made no new advances on Emily and kept things strictly on a friendly basis. He was amazing with Trevor and spent hours each day with him. Trevor was even starting to ride on his own.

She wanted to find the courage to ask Chris on a real date, but she was a bit old-fashioned and believed the man should ask the woman out. When he didn't ask, she was disappointed, but certainly not devastated. She wasn't particularly attracted to him; she just wanted to get her focus off Mark.

It wasn't helping to be living in Mark's home, seeing him daily, and spending time with his family, as well. He was too everything — too masculine, too friendly, too good with animals and kids. He was just too much.

Every time she looked at her young man with Mark, however, it reinforced her decision to fight the attraction she had for him. She had to keep it professional because, if she started a relationship with Mark, when it ended, she and Trevor would have to move. That would be too painful for her son.

It wasn't as if she had to worry about a relationship, though, as the man hadn't shown any further personal interest in her. She and Trevor had been at the ranch for a full month, and Mark hadn't touched her once since that steamy night, a night that now seemed so long ago.

What irritated her was that she *wanted* him to touch her. She was grateful nothing had escalated, because she didn't think she was strong enough to tell him no.

His family came up a couple of times more, and she was becoming good friends with Jessica and Amy. Even if she didn't stay on at the ranch, Emily knew the three of them would remain friends for a long time to come — that was, if she didn't have to leave the state of Washington. Being on the run didn't make keeping friendships very easy.

Since she'd always had a hard time opening up with people, it was even worse to like these women so much. It would hurt to grow close to them and then have to leave suddenly. Still, since she hadn't heard anything from her ex-in-laws in months, she was starting to feel more secure.

Maybe they hadn't found her yet. But maybe, just maybe, they'd finally given up and were allowing her to live her life with her son. They didn't love him. She knew that was a terrible thing to think, but the entire time she'd been with her husband, they hadn't wanted anything to do with Trevor or her. They'd doted on their son, but she and Trevor might as well have been pieces of furniture in their eyes.

They were just mean, terrible people, in her humble opinion, and she couldn't believe she was even doing them the courtesy of thinking about them.

Emily finally had a real spa day scheduled the following weekend. She'd never done anything of that sort, and it sounded like heaven. To have real girlfriends and a day to pamper herself seemed unreal. Most kids got to do things like that during high school, but she'd been too tomboyish to spend money frivolously on girly things.

It was kind of funny how you changed as you aged. When she was fifteen, she had enjoyed playing sports, sliding into home plate in the mud, and doing anything physical. As she got older, she cared more about doing her hair, taking a bit of time with her makeup, and trying to be a little more feminine.

Growing up, her best friends had always been males. She hadn't started thinking of them in a sexual way until about the time she'd graduated from high school. Her parents were probably exceedingly grateful for that, considering how many high school pregnancies there had been in her senior class.

No. For her, it had been sports and more sports. She rather missed a dirty game of baseball. Somehow she couldn't see Amy and Jessica playing a game with her, but maybe she could talk some of the ranch hands into it.

Now wasn't the time to think like a tomboy, however; now was time to think of girly stuff. It was OK to be both feminine and sporty, she decided as she thought about her upcoming girl time.

With her resolve set, Emily pulled her gaze from the window where Mark and Trevor were rolling around on the lawn with the ever-growing puppies. She focused on cooking, which always eased her tension.

She was in a good place. No more thinking inappropriate thoughts of Mark, and no more taking the easy way out. She was building a new life for herself and she wasn't going to live in fear of what tomorrow would bring.

Pushing thoughts of her life in California from her head, she got back to making dinner, with the sound of her son and Mark laughing providing the music that she cooked to.

Chapter Eleven

Claustrophobia in a bedroom the size of Montana? It
made no sense, but no one expected phobias to make
sense, Emily said to herself and laughed quietly.
Things had just snowballed. First the anxieties,
rational and less rational, that had kept her tossing
and turning for more than an hour. Then, as she'd
grown more exhausted and her thoughts had festered,
she could feel even the blankets take on a threatening
aspect. They'd been clutching at her feet, and then
she was trapped! Enter full-blown panic attack, stage
right.

She'd struggled free from those ridiculous bed
demons and staggered out to her balcony, grabbing
her sheer robe as she moved, and putting it on. And
now she was feeling much calmer as she leaned
against the railing and breathed in the fresh country
air. Her panic attack fled into the night sky, and her
remaining anxieties — nothing. Gone.

"What are you doing out here?"

Emily jumped at least a foot off the balcony floor as she spun around to see Mark standing a few feet away from her. *He could have had the decency to be wearing a bit more than just a pair of boxer shorts. They were showing far more than they hid, for heaven's sake.*

"I...I...just needed some air," she finally managed to stutter.

Mark couldn't take his eyes off of her. He was looking at her from head to toe and taking his sweet time about it. It was a full moon that night, and she was wearing an almost see-through short nightie and iridescent robe. *She was displaying more of her body than she did in her bikini. Sheesh.* The moonlight seemed to turn the white material iridescent.

He could see the dusky outline of her nipples, which hardened to peaks as his eyes roved over them. The outline of her legs went all the way up to her most intimate of places. Before he knew what he was doing, he was walking toward her.

He was slow and steady as he took those few paces that separated them. Her eyes never wavered from his as he made his approach. It was as if they were both in some inescapable trance. He reached his hand up and brushed back the tendrils of hair floating free in her face.

She couldn't contain a sigh when his fingers made contact with her burning flesh. She started leaning toward him in an unspoken invitation. That was all the prompting he needed.

He wrapped one arm around her back, pulling her tightly against his nearly naked body. The other hand wrapped around the back of her neck, tilting her head up, giving him access to her full lips.

He gave her a moment more to turn him away. It would kill him if she denied him, but he'd die rather than use force. When the moan escaped her moistened lips, he finally brought his lips down to hers.

She had thought the kiss would be urgent, like the one in the pool, but was surprised when his lips barely brushed hers. She moaned again and raised her hands to grip his neck, pulling him closer to her. She wanted to feel him pressed against her in every single way. She had no time for regrets; she wanted him and she needed him to kiss her fully and take the ache away.

Giving them what they both desired, he crushed her lips beneath his. He tilted his head, opening her mouth wider, so he could slip his tongue inside. Their tongues mated as their hips ground together, heating them both up for the inevitable conclusion.

He let out a moan as she pushed her softness into his engorged manhood. His hand ran down the round perfection of her backside until it found the hem of her nightgown. Then he slowly inched his way up her silken thighs until he was gripping her, pulling her even tighter against him.

He let out another long moan as he realized she wore nothing under the wisp of a nightgown. The only thing separating him from entering her right then was the extremely thin cotton of his boxer shorts.

He suddenly swung his arm under her thighs, picking her up in his arms. He never broke contact from the passionate kiss they were sharing. Carrying her the few feet to his balcony door, he walked to his bed, where he gently laid her down.

He stripped off his boxers and then her thin robe in two quick motions and lay next to her on the soft comforter. His hands roamed across her body, compelled to touch everywhere, and never touching her enough for him. He found every one of her pleasure points and almost ended things before they had begun when her cry of pleasure nearly shattered his control.

He tore his lips from hers so he could trail them down her smooth throat. He licked and nipped at her erratically beating pulse and then made his way down to her generous breasts. *So curvy, so beautiful.* Her dusky pink nipples were beaded and shining in the moonlight. He licked around their hardened peaks before drawing first one and then the other deep into his mouth.

Emily arched off the bed as he continued to lick and suck his way slowly down her torso. He circled her slight belly button and then moved lower. As his hands kneaded her thighs and his teeth grazed her skin, she cried out more and more. Then he gently soothed her flesh with the flick of his tongue.

When he finally spread her legs apart and kissed her in her most sacred place, she begged him to love her. "Please, Mark, please... I need you inside me," she cried. With one more flick of his masterful tongue, her entire body jerked up, and sweet heavenly release washed throughout her.

She couldn't have even lifted her head; the pleasure was so encompassing. He slowly kissed his way back up her body and flicked her still tender nipples, eliciting from her a surprised moan. She didn't understand how she could possibly need or want any more pleasure, but as he brought their mouths back together, desire burned hot inside her once more.

Mark quickly sheathed himself, grateful for the protection nearby. Then he lay on top of her, pressing himself against her heat.

Emily could feel him throbbing against her aching core. She opened up her legs wider so he could finally join their bodies together, but he still held back.

He ran his hands down over her hips and then teased her aching nub as his tongue danced with hers. Fully and desperately aroused now, she lifted her hips up, begging with her body for him to take her. She couldn't believe that the whimpers she heard were coming from her own throat.

He slipped his finger inside her, testing her body, seeing whether she was ready for him. When he felt she was as ready as he was, he finally stopped the torture, and in one swift thrust, he was deep inside her. She cried out in pleasure and ground her hips to his. She wanted more.

"Give me one minute," Mark begged her.

Emily felt a power unlike anything she'd ever felt in her life. She'd made this big, strong man beg *her* for mercy. It was a euphoric feeling, and she wiggled her hips again and smiled as she saw the sweat bead on his forehead.

He saw her smile and matched it with a wicked one of his own. "You're quite the tease, aren't you?"

That was something she'd never been called before. To her surprise, she rather liked the experience.

He then began thrusting in and out of her with speed, and there was no way she could have squeezed any words past her tightened throat, let alone thought another thought. He held her close as he kissed her, rhythmically thrusting in and out of her body. She lost all sense of time, dizzy in the immense feelings building higher and higher inside her.

He thrust in again, and her body convulsed around him as her pleasure seemed to stretch on and on. With a groan, he pushed into her one last time before he gave a final shudder and then collapsed on top of her. They were both breathing heavily, and neither had any energy to move.

He finally shifted their bodies so that she was half on top of him and half lying next to him. Fumbling with the protection, he quickly got rid of it, then pulled her tightly against him. He was unwilling to let her go. He brought the cover up to keep the chilled night air off her body and closed his eyes, enjoying the feel of her warming his skin. He didn't know why he'd fought against this all month.

"I should go," she said sleepily, though she didn't try to move.

"Not yet."

She didn't have any energy to argue with him and told herself she'd get up in a few moments. She would allow herself to rest her eyes for a minute. They were so heavy, and she couldn't seem to keep them open.

Chapter Twelve

Emily eased her eyes open and stretched her sore muscles. At first, she was confused by the stiffness of her body, and then the night came back to her like cold water splashed in her face. She sat straight up in the unfamiliar room and looked around.

Mark wasn't there, and she was incredibly grateful for that. She needed time to gather herself together before she faced him. She'd never before made love to a man she wasn't in a relationship with. In fact, before Mark, she'd only been with her husband, and sex had never been a quarter as good with that adulterous louse as it had been with Mark.

She'd fallen asleep in his arms, only to be awakened sometime in the night by his roving hands. He had loved her again, giving her more pleasure, and then she'd fallen into a sleep so good that no dreams had dared intrude.

She found her nightgown on the floor near the bed, and she slipped it over her head. She then walked to the doors and peeked out at the balcony. No one was out there, or anywhere in the backyard, so she quickly ran to her own bedroom door. She felt like a thief sneaking into the house, silently, suspiciously, guiltily.

She hadn't known Mark's room was so close to hers. If she'd known that sooner, she would have had an even harder time falling asleep at night. Would she ever be able sleep again with this new knowledge?

Emily allowed herself an extra-long shower, seeking relief for her aches and pains. She'd used muscles she hadn't known existed. But, though her body was sore, she reveled in the feeling.

She had to smile as she thought back to the intense pleasure Mark had brought her. But reality came calling while she got dressed. She would have to tell him that the night had been wonderful but it couldn't continue. She loved working for him, and that was far more important than some fling — even a deliciously fulfilling fling that was unlike anything she'd ever known.

It sounded rational to her, and she hoped he wouldn't take it as rejection. She certainly couldn't tell him it had been the best sex she'd ever had in her life. That wasn't the way to get him not to want any more of it. Then again, he was a virile, handsome, amazing man. What had been spectacular for her had probably been the norm for him. When she asked that things return to the way they'd been, she was sure he'd just shrug his shoulders and say, "Fine."

Emily's confidence was returning when she finally descended the stairs. She walked into the kitchen and found Trevor and Mark sitting at table, each with a large bowl of cereal before them. They both looked up guiltily, as if they'd been caught doing something wrong.

Emily thought that was strange until she noticed the cereal the two of them were polishing off was Cookie Crisp. She never let her son eat such cereal, and always told him she might as well just give him a spoon and let him eat right out of the sugar bowl.

She was close to scolding Trevor for eating something he knew he wasn't supposed to, but the look on their faces was just too pathetic. She couldn't keep a smile from slipping through.

"Don't get used to eating this" was all she said. She grabbed a bowl and poured the very small amount left in the box for herself. *Hmmm. Not bad.* But she wouldn't admit that to the smug boys staring at her. "I'm only eating this so you two won't have any more," she insisted.

Mark let a small chuckle escape. She glared in response, then finished her breakfast. He was eating the cereal as fast as he could, the way he ate everything. You might have thought the man grew up in an orphanage, the way he ate.

"Why do you always eat so quickly?" she finally asked, her curiosity getting the better of her.

"If you'd grown up with two older brothers, you'd eat fast too," he mumbled around the bite in his mouth.

Emily chuckled at the image of Lucas and Alex filching Mark's food. He smiled at her, and she almost forgot they needed to have a serious conversation later.

"Mom, don't forget I'm going to the movie today with Jasmine," Trevor said through gulps of his chocolate milk.

"Oh, I did forget. Finish up so we can get you dressed. Lucas will be here any time," she said while starting to clear away dishes from the table.

"I'm done," Trevor said and then dashed up the stairs. He liked nothing more than to spend time with Jasmine, who had become his new best friend.

"Wait for me," Emily said as she chased after her son. She quickly got him ready to go, and by the time they started downstairs, she could hear Jasmine calling for him.

"I'm here, Jazzy," Trevor yelled from the top of the stairs and then jumped on the railing and made the long slide down. Emily stared dumbfounded.

"Trevor, you may not slide on the rail," she scolded her son. "Whatever gave you that idea?"

Trevor looked up at her guiltily and then shrugged his shoulders.

"It's my fault, Emily," Mark piped up. "I'm sorry. I kind of showed him how to do it."

Emily turned her astonished gaze on Mark. She then threw her hands in the air in defeat. She couldn't understand men. The banister was beautiful and expensive, and they were using it as a slide. She decided to let it go. Sometimes that was the smartest thing to do.

"There you are," Jasmine said as they came around the corner. "I missed you." She grabbed Trevor up in a hug. He hugged her back, and they exchanged goofy grins.

How sweet they are together, Emily thought.

"Is it OK if Trevor stays the night?" Lucas asked Emily. "We're going to be done with the park and movie late, and I'm sure they'll have a good time."

"If you honestly don't think it will be a problem."

"Are you kidding me? He's a great kid. I really enjoy having him come over; plus, it's the only time I can get Jasmine to stop talking," he whispered.

Emily chuckled and then kissed her son goodbye. She reminded him to listen to Lucas and Amy, and to be on his best behavior.

Lucas took off, and suddenly, Emily was alone with Mark. Well, she told herself, there was no time like the present to have their conversation.

"Mark, we need to talk."

"I was afraid you were going to say that."

"Last night was magical. It was the best night I have ever had."

"Well that sounds like a great conversation. I say we end before you add in a *but…*" he started to say.

"I wish it were that simple, Mark, but we both know we can't let it happen again. Trevor is so happy here, and you know this thing between us won't last. Then everything will fall apart." She spoke in pleading tones.

"Why can't it last?" he asked.

"Mark, you're my boss. You're amazing, and your family is incredible, and I don't want to have an affair and then end up with the two of us not liking each other. Can't we please be thankful we had a great night together and now call it good?"

Mark stared into her eyes for several moments before letting out a long sigh. "I'm not happy about this, and I guarantee you, I'll try to change your mind, but if you need me to back off for now, then that's what I'll do," he finally conceded.

Emily felt the breath in her chest pressing in. Why did he have to always say the right things? Why did he have to seem so perfect? She was sure Mark Anderson had faults, but as of yet, she sure hadn't been able to discover any of them — well, besides teaching her son bad habits, but, dang it, even that was endearing.

"Thank you. Can we please go back to the way things have been?"

"I need to go work out in the barn for a while" was his only answer. He walked out the back door and left her feeling a bit rejected.

If this was all for the best, why did she feel so miserable? Sometimes it would have been so much easier to be a child and not have the reservations you developed as you got older. She knew she was doing the right thing; she just had to keep convincing herself of that.

She didn't see Mark the rest of the day. They both were managing to avoid each other, and that was good.

Chapter Thirteen

Everyone else was gone. Even Edward was off visiting with his daughter, and that left just Mark and her. And it was driving her crazy. Emily knew Mark was watching a movie in the den, and she felt an unbelievable pull to join him on the couch, curl up against his side and forget what she'd said to him earlier.

He had respected her wishes, had even worked the entire day out in the barn. But she was having a heck of a time keeping her end of the bargain up.

She decided to take a stroll out to the stream running behind the barns. The yard was well lit, and she'd yet to feel fear taking her solitary rambles. Mark had men guarding his animals twenty-four hours a day, so even if someone managed to get onto the property, all she'd have to do was let out a scream, and someone would come running.

As she moved through the cool grass, her toes exposed from the thin pair of sandals she was wearing, she felt a little of the tension begin to ease.

Yes. She'd just *had* to get out of the house. Her claustrophobia had returned, this time in a place that was at least eight thousand square feet. It was almost comical. There were places in the home she hadn't even seen yet.

When she'd been there longer, she would start exploring more, opening some of the doors she'd been curious about. Maybe Mark had some fetishes that he kept behind locked doors. The thought made her giggle.

She almost hoped the perfect man had a few demons hiding in his closets, though certainly not Bluebeard's wives. Then maybe she'd get over this awkward infatuation.

"What are you doing out here so late?"

Emily jumped at the sound of another voice. Slowly she turned and breathed a sigh of relief at the sight of Chris.

"I'm just taking a walk. I needed some fresh air," she said as she stepped onto the dock and moved to the end. Chris followed, keeping a respectable distance between them.

"Is everything all right?"

"Yes, it's fine. I always find myself at a loss when Trevor isn't with me," she said. It was regrettable how much her world revolved around her only child. What would she do when he was all grown up and had moved away?

"Where's Trevor? Your son rarely leaves."

"He's spending the night at Jasmine's. They went to the zoo today and then had a movie marathon. I talked to him for about two seconds before he told me he was too busy to talk right then, and he handed the phone back to Amy," she said with a sigh.

"They sure grow quickly," he agreed.

"Do you have children, Chris?" She'd never thought to ask. A man his age could easily have a kid or two out there, maybe living with their mother. For that matter, he could be married. She'd never even considered it.

Without thinking much about it, she glanced down at his left hand, but there wasn't a ring or a white patch where one may have rested that he'd quickly removed.

"No. No kids yet, but I wouldn't mind a couple, especially if they're as good as Trevor," he said with a grin, and she had no doubt that he was flirting with her.

She knew she should flirt back, put in some effort toward finally getting that offer of a date. But, after spending the night in Mark's bed last night, she couldn't make herself do it. It was just too soon. Not to mention a little tacky.

"I've been very blessed with Trevor. He's the kind of child parents dream of having," she said, careful to keep the focus on her son and not herself.

"What are you doing this weekend?" he asked. She didn't know whether he was leading up to asking her out, or if he was just casually asking. This was where she should let him know she was open to an invitation, but no matter how she tried, she couldn't get the words past her throat to give him hope.

Finally she gave up. "I'm going with Amy and Jessica to the spa. I've never been, so it should be pretty amazing."

Emily trailed her feet off the dock and felt the icy-cold water begin to numb her toes. It was perfect for keeping her alert.

"That's too bad. I heard there's going to be a great country band in town," he said.

From the tone of his voice, she really couldn't tell where he was going with all of this. Should she be flattered? Was he leading up to asking her out? She really was no good with the flirting thing.

"Oh, I do love live music. Maybe I'll be able to catch them the next time they come around," she said a bit evasively. She wanted to leave the door open…just in case.

"Yeah, me and the boys go in every weekend. We all love the ranch, but when the weekend hits, it's nice to kick up our feet," he said, laughing.

"I can't imagine there's a job out there where men work harder than cowboys do. You guys pull long days and nights and sure put your bodies through the ringer. I'm seriously impressed." she said.

"It's certainly a good workout. I'm in the best shape of my life," he said with a wink her way as he held up an arm and flexed. Emily couldn't help but laugh.

"That's good…I guess," she said with a smile.

"It sure beats being one of those schmucks who have to sit at a desk all day."

"I don't know. I think different things appeal to different people. I know when I was younger, I would much rather be outside chasing some sort of ball or other, but now I really enjoy working in a kitchen all day. Who knows what I will love to do in another ten years?"

"Well, we're all sure grateful you love the kitchen. The food here is the best I've ever eaten," he said.

"Thank you, Chris. I'm glad you appreciate it so much. I'll have to make you boys some extra goodies to take to the bunkhouse."

"I don't want to make you work harder, but I sure as heck won't turn an offer like that down."

"Well, then, I'll get on it first thing in the morning."

"So, it seems that you and the boss have been getting nice and cozy," he said as if in passing. She instantly tensed.

"I like Mark. He's a good man to work for, but there's nothing going on between us," she insisted.

He looked at her as if he knew something, but he didn't challenge her. Emily thought about the kiss on the balcony last night —well, a great deal more had happened than kissing. Mark's hands had been all over her body before he'd lifted her in his arms and carried her inside.

That someone might have spotted them had never crossed her mind. The balcony had been dark, only the moonlight offering a little illumination. It had been late. Surely no one had seen them and then spoke of it. The thought was mortifying.

"I'd best be getting to bed. Six in the morning comes awfully early," Chris said, his voice still pleasant as he rose to his feet. "Do you want me to walk back with you?"

"No, but thank you. Have a good night, Chris." She breathed a sigh of relief as he walked away.

Emily sat there for another fifteen minutes, and then suddenly was filled with chills. She glanced around, having the feeling that someone was watching her. Suddenly her little walk had turned uncomfortable, and she stood up, the peacefulness of the night shattered.

She looked all around her as she began moving quickly up the path back to the house. Surely it was all in her head. Mark's property was safe.

When she reached the back porch and glanced out at the yard, she still couldn't shake the thought of someone out there with his or her eyes on her. It made her heart thunder and her knees a little shaky.

Stepping inside, she locked the back door, then quickly made her way through the halls to the stairs. She didn't feel any easier until she was safely in her bedroom. She was sure it was nothing other than her imagination, and her fear that someone had spotted her and Mark on the balcony the night before.

By the time she finally managed to fall asleep, dawn was starting to approach. It looked as if she'd have a very exhausting day when she had to rise in a few hours.

Chapter Fourteen

Progress, and it took only a few weeks — Emily and Mark could be in the same room once again without too much tension. They'd even gone back to some of their earlier teasing.

Emily was feeling more secure each day. She'd still find her eyes drawn to Mark, and she always seemed to know where he was, but she cared far too much about him to risk losing him with a cheap romance.

Her body ached each night, wanting him with a desire she'd never known before, but she was used to denying herself for the sake of others. In this case, she was putting her son's needs ahead of her own, which made the sacrifice worth it. She at least thought it was worth it, or hoped it was.

What made the aching even worse was that every day that she was around Mark, she fell a little bit more in love with him. How could she not love a man who was so gentle with her son and so compassionate to all those around him? He was even a saint when it came to his animals.

She had yet to find a single flaw. She didn't understand how he wasn't already married with ten kids. He would make the perfect husband and father, and she'd had her own dreams, more than once, on that score.

Emily and Trevor were playing a game of Candy Land in the den when Mark came in. "Mark, look: I'm beating my mom again," Trevor said, beaming at his hero.

"Great job, buddy. Edward just brought in some chocolate cake. If you hurry to the kitchen, you can get some before he puts it away," he said.

"Yea," Trevor yelled and took off running down the hallway.

"You know you're spoiling him," Emily admonished, but the smile she gave him took away any sting.

"I really love having him here. He brings so much light to the house."

"Thank you for caring so much about my son," Emily said as tears stung her eyes.

"Emily, we need to talk about Trevor's school. The year starts in a few weeks." Mark started out carefully. He was prepared for a minor battle with the stubborn mother.

"There's a great school here. I was going to go talk to them next week," she said, thinking the discussion would be over.

"Lucas told me all about the school Jasmine's enrolled in, and it's not much farther from this area. He would have a lot of opportunities there that you can't get from a public school, and he'd get to go with Jasmine," he told her.

"Mark, I simply can't afford to place Trevor in a private school."

"You wouldn't have to pay anything. It would be a part of your employment."

"There's no way I can accept that, Mark. You already sneak things to Trevor all the time, like the dirt bike you got him last week. He will be fine going to the local school here," she said stubbornly. She already owed Mark so much and didn't want to be indebted to him any further.

Mark was prepared for her argument. He'd already discovered she wasn't a greedy person. As a matter of fact, she was the complete opposite. It was downright frustrating trying to give her or her son anything.

"Just let me explain myself before you start getting all defensive and completely close the discussion off," he began.

"Fine. Go ahead and explain yourself, but I'm telling you the answer will still be *no*. You're wasting your time," she said, crossing her arms.

"You are the most infuriating woman. I also said not to get all defensive," he almost shouted.

They both stared, neither willing to back down. Emily finally folded and shrugged her shoulders. "Go ahead," she mumbled, but she was only humoring him. She wasn't going to allow him to pay for her son to go to private school. That was out of the question.

"Thank you. As I was saying, the school is top of the line, and if Trevor went there, he would be provided with far more opportunities than a public school could give him. The public school system has had too many budget cuts. Heck, he wouldn't even be able to learn another language or participate in any good clubs. Those are things he really needs to secure his future."

"But the money…" she began.

Mark held his hand up. "You can talk to many different employees, some of mine and some of the Anderson Corporation. We have added benefits where we pay for college tuition and extended leaves. We believe in taking care of our own. I paid for Edward's kids to go to college, and he didn't fight me on it, so please put Trevor above your pride and allow him to take this opportunity," he said. He knew that last bit was a low blow, but he also knew that she was willing to make just about any sacrifice for her son, even if that sacrifice was accepting something from another person.

Emily sat, fighting with herself. She knew she could be hurting her son's future success by not letting him go to the better school, but she didn't want to be in any further debt to Mark.

"I can understand your points, and you are right," she finally conceded.

Mark looked a bit smug at her words. She held her hand up to let him know she wasn't finished speaking, and his smile instantly vanished.

"I said I can understand your point; however, if you expect me to compromise, you need to be willing to also," she said, staring him in the eye to make sure she was getting her point across.

"What kind of compromise?" he asked suspiciously.

"If Trevor is attending a fancy school, then I insist on contributing to it. We already have no expenses here, zero, and I receive a generous salary. I'm sure the tuition is a lot, so you'll cut my salary in half." She thought that would make an acceptable solution for them both.

"No way," Mark told her, with no room for compromise on his part.

"Then it's no deal," Emily said, just as unbending as he was.

They both stared again at each other again, to see who blinked first. When Emily refused to back down, Mark finally held up his hands in defeat.

"OK, how about your salary gets cut by one hundred a week, not half?" he said.

When she started to shake her head, he cut her off. "Listen, if he's going to a private school, there are extra things you are going to need. You'll need your salary."

Emily hadn't even thought about the added expenses. Mark wasn't going to tell her about the extra fees for field trips and such. He would just make sure the school contacted him directly, because if she knew any of that, she would insist on breaking herself to pay them. He didn't understand her scruples; he wouldn't miss the money at all. He was frustrated with her and at the same time impressed with her independence.

"I guess we could try it out," she conceded reluctantly. "But, Mark, if the kids there make him feel bad about himself because he's not rich like they are, he's not staying. I would rather he have a public school education than for him to ever feel like he isn't good enough."

"Emily, he'll fit right in. He already has a best friend he'll be going to school with, and he's outgoing and social. He'll be friends with every kid in the school," he promised her.

"OK, when does registration start?" she asked.

"We can go up there tomorrow. We'll take the chopper over to my dad's and then drive in. I've been promising Trevor for a while to take him on a ride."

"I think it would be just fine to drive," she said nervously. She was terrified of heights and not a fan of flying in anything, let alone a tiny helicopter, which remained in the air solely because of a couple of steel bars spinning around.

"Don't be such a chicken. You'll love the view, and it's only about a fifteen-minute ride, but we'll probably take the scenic route," he added with a wink.

Emily shuddered and resigned herself to new adventures.

Chapter Fifteen

"Come on, Mom. It's time to go," Trevor said, pacing around her bedroom while she finished the last touches of her makeup.

"I'm hurrying," she lied.

"Mark said you're dragging your feet because you're afraid to go in the helicopter," Trevor said.

"Well, Mark doesn't know everything."

"Yes, he does, Mom," Trevor said, as if she had lost her mind. "He's the smartest guy in the whole wide world."

Emily cleared her throat to keep from laughing and followed her son out of the room. She really was terrified to go on the chopper, but she absolutely refused to admit that to either her son or Mark. They would both tease her mercilessly.

"All ready?" Mark asked when they reached the bottom of the stairs. Emily glared at him as he tried to wipe the wide grin from his face. When he started to cough, she wasn't fooled into thinking he wasn't laughing at her.

"I just think it's silly to fly there when it's not that long a car ride," Emily had to say. She knew it was a lost battle, but she had to try one more time to change his mind.

"Ah, Mom, you're just no fun."

"Don't worry, Trevor. She'll have a great time once we're up in the air. I'm an excellent pilot," Mark told him.

"You're flying it?" Emily gasped in horror.

"Do you see any other pilots around here?" Mark said.

"I just assumed you'd have one come in," Emily said. She'd hoped he would, anyway. She knew he could ride a horse better than anyone she knew, but she wasn't so sure he was capable of keeping her and her son up in the air in a flying deathtrap.

"Don't worry; I have plenty of hours flying. You're in safe hands," he said with a wink. She wasn't reassured one bit, but it was too late to back out now. Maybe she could fake an illness. One look at her son's face, and she knew she was stuck.

"Let's go; daylight is wasting," Mark called. Trevor was on his heels as they headed out the back door and toward the helicopter pad.

Emily followed at a much more sedate pace, still dragging her feet. When they got to the helicopter and she saw it up close for the first time, her fear kicked into overdrive. She worried she might end up passing out on the flight. Of course, if that happened, it would be over that much sooner.

After he did a pre-trip inspection of the aircraft, Mark helped Trevor inside and got him buckled. The boy grinned hugely when Mark put the headphones on his head and explained that they could talk back and forth through the built-in microphones.

"Ready?" he asked Emily when she was still staring in the door.

"I guess so," she answered, slowly stepping forward.

Mark placed his hands on her hips and boosted her inside. Emily felt goose bumps rise as his hands lingered on her for a moment longer than necessary. When he settled her in the seat, their mouths were only a couple of inches apart.

She nearly fainted at the instant heat flaming in his eyes. He continued to stare at her for a few more moments before handing her the headset and then shutting her door. She let out the breath she hadn't even realized she was holding and was surprised by the disappointment she felt when he hadn't closed the gap and kissed her.

She didn't have time to feel sorry for herself, however, because Mark had jumped in the pilot's seat and started the propellers, and she was focused on nothing but her fear. As the helicopter began to rise straight up into the air, she was once again holding her breath. The higher they got, the more she sweated.

She couldn't believe she'd let them talk her into this. She was thinking about demanding to be put back on solid ground when they shot out across the countryside.

"Wow, Mark, this is the coolest thing ever," she heard her son say into the microphone. The sound of her son's excitement abated a little bit of her panic. He was in heaven riding shotgun next to Mark.

"The first time up is the greatest, but it's still pretty cool even after hundreds of times," Mark said. She saw him reach over and ruffle Trevor's hair.

"Mom's just silly. There's nothing to be scared of," Trevor said bravely.

"Careful, young man; your mom can hear us," Mark said and then looked back at her and winked. She was more horrified by the fact that he'd looked away from the front window than by anything they were saying.

"Sorry, Mom."

"It's OK; you're just braver than I am," she replied.

"That's OK, Mom. Guys are supposed to take care of their special women," Trevor said in all seriousness. "Isn't that right, Mark?"

"Sure is, Trevor."

"Oh, yeah? Am I your special lady?" Emily replied with a big smile. Trevor laughed while giving her a quick nod.

Emily was so proud of her son. He really was growing up fast. He was already a gentleman. She knew there wouldn't be a woman out there who'd ever be good enough for him.

Emily finally realized that while she'd been talking to Trevor, her fear had started to dissipate, and she even began taking in the scenery below. She was shocked to find she was starting to enjoy the thrill of being so high up and yet close enough to see all the buildings and fields.

As she gazed from the window, she watched as the fields with animals and large farmhouses began to get closer together, and then they were flying over the city. Seattle truly was a thing of beauty with its crisscrossing freeways and its huge buildings trying to reach the sky. What made it all so much better was all the water surrounding it, and the view of mountains so close, she felt as if she could reach out and grab them.

There was no way she was going to admit to Mark she was starting to enjoy the ride. She sat back and drank in the view while listening to Mark and Trevor talk back and forth. They were speaking a little more guardedly than before.

Almost before the ride had started, they were making their descent. "Is something wrong?" she asked with concern.

"We've arrived at my father's," Mark said.

"That really was fast," she replied.

"We've been in the air about thirty minutes. I told you I was taking the scenic route," he said smugly.

She glared at the back of his head. He sounded way too smug. Well, he could *think* she'd enjoyed the ride, but she wouldn't confirm it. That comforted her somewhat.

She looked over the lands as they were approaching and was once again awestruck. The house that sat centered in their view made Mark's place look small. It seemed like a castle, with its rising towers and brick exterior, and she looked around, expecting to see a moat and drawbridge. The image made her giggle. Mark was most certainly a man she could imagine rescuing a princess from a tower.

When she'd thought about money before, she'd pictured her ex-in-laws. They used their money to lord over other people and look down on the masses. But they'd be considered poor compared with the Andersons, who were of the people and for the people.

They landed smoothly, much to Emily's relief, and Mark turned the chopper off. They all climbed out and headed up the hill to the mansion. Joseph came out to greet them about halfway.

"Hi, little man; did you enjoy the ride?" Joseph asked.

"It was the funnest thing ever!" Trevor exclaimed.

"Most fun," Emily automatically corrected her son.

"Aw, Mom," Trevor complained. She let it go.

"Do you want some breakfast before you head off to your new school?" Joseph asked.

"Sure," he said and followed Joseph up to the house, with Emily and Mark right behind.

"How did you enjoy the ride?" Joseph asked Emily.

"It was fine."

"She was scared," Trevor piped in.

Joseph chuckled as Emily's face took on a grim aspect. "It's OK, young lady; my son is a bit frightening."

"Thanks, Dad," Mark said, with the hint of a blush.

"You and your brothers would upset your mom all the time with your daredevil ways. I don't think she got a full night's rest all the years you were growing up."

"Well, who taught us those dangerous activities?" Mark asked with a pointed look.

"There's no use in pointing fingers," he grumbled and changed the subject.

Emily decided to say nothing.

They had a wonderful breakfast at the house and then drove to the school to get Trevor registered. Emily was pleasantly surprised by the place. It was large but not overwhelmingly so, and the staffers were friendly. Not one of them seemed to look down on her or her son.

Of course, it never occurred to her that she was there with Mark Anderson. Maybe that was a big reason the women there were being so kind, and trying to get as close as possible to her.

When they got to Trevor's classroom, Jasmine came running around the corner. "You're finally here," she said and gave Trevor a big hug.

"I got to fly with Mark."

"Oh, that's so much fun," Jasmine cried. The two children chatted faster than Emily could keep up with them.

"Mrs. Parson, this is my cousin, Trevor," Jasmine said and dragged him over to the teacher.

Emily stopped what she was doing and looked guiltily over at Mark, who hadn't even seemed to notice anything was wrong. Lucas was talking with his brother, and neither of them gave the slightest indication they'd heard anything. She was grateful. She would have to pull Trevor aside later and explain to him again that Mark was just her boss and they weren't related to Jasmine. How did you break a young man's heart, though? Maybe it wasn't that big a deal, but she didn't want her son to think they were a family and going to live together forever. What would happen to him then if they had to move? It would break his heart.

She would have to think about what she was doing and what was best for her son. She didn't want to leave, but she knew she'd better make sure Trevor knew Mark was the employer and not a substitute father.

They visited the school for a few hours and got Trevor signed up for class, and Emily was feeling pretty good about letting him attend. The place did have some impressive programs that she knew he wouldn't get from a public school; the field trips alone were spectacular.

"We are going school shopping now, Emily; please tell me you can come with us," Amy said as they were all heading out of the school.

"I guess that's up to Mark," Emily said and looked over at him.

"In that case, it's a definite yes," Amy said as she dragged Emily behind her. "Let's take our car so we can chat and let the guys do all the driving," she added enthusiastically.

Emily had an incredible day. She purchased new clothes and school supplies for Trevor and enjoyed lunch at Chuck E. Cheese's, watching the guys compete with the kids in the games. She laughed so much that, by the end of the day, her stomach hurt.

"I'm so glad the kids are going to the same school. We'll have to chaperone together so we can see each other all the time," Amy said as they were getting ready to leave.

"I was already thinking I would love to chaperone those field trips. I'll be more excited to go to the places than Trevor will be," Emily added shyly.

"Me, too," Amy exclaimed. "These guys are used to all this fun stuff, but I still can't get enough of the amazing world around me," she added.

Emily loved that she and Amy had so much in common. It gave her hope in humanity to see someone who had so much be so sweet and genuinely great to be around.

"I'll see you soon," Emily said and hugged Amy goodbye.

By the time they got back to the ranch, the sun was starting to set. Trevor was rubbing his eyes, and Mark carried him up to his room. Emily quickly got him ready for bed and then barely managed to drag herself to her room. It had been a wonderful day, and she felt her life was finally starting to be normal.

Chapter Sixteen

"Mom, I'm leaving now," Trevor said, snapping Emily out of her daydream.

"Sorry, Trevor; I lost track of time." She gave him a big kiss and walked out the front door with him. He climbed into the car with Edward, and he waved as she stood silently watching them drive away until they were out of sight.

It was Trevor's second week at his school, and he couldn't wait to get out the door each morning. He loved the place so much and always came home telling her the fantastic things he'd done.

She headed inside and finished making breakfast for all the hands. They'd started coming in earlier each day and were usually there about an hour before the actual meal was ready. She loved to talk with them and started preparing some fruit and breads the night before so they had things to munch on while waiting for their hot food.

"Emily, I think I've gained ten pounds since you became our cook. Pretty soon, I'm not going to be able to button my jeans anymore," one of her favorite ranch hands said. He leaned back in his chair and groaned.

"I don't think you could gain a single pound, considering how hard you work. You need your fuel for the day."

"I think I'm in love with you," John said and gave her an adoring smile.

"You're in love with my cooking skills."

"Come on, Emily, run away with me," he teased her.

"John, don't make me call your mom. She wouldn't be happy to hear that her eighteen-year-old son was hitting on an older woman," she teased.

"Heck, she would tell me how smart I was," he replied.

"John, don't make me put you on muck duty all day," Mark said as he entered the room. He ruffled the ranch hand's hair.

"I'm trying to convince Emily to run away with me. She's being stubborn, though," John said with a full-blown grin at Mark and then Emily.

"If anyone is going to try to convince Emily to run away with him, it will be me," Mark said in a teasing voice but with a serious look in his eyes.

"OK, no more chocolate muffins for you guys in the morning. It makes you all too rowdy. Now go get to work," Emily said and pushed all the men out of the kitchen. "I will see you at lunch."

She watched the men fondly as they made their way toward the barn. She cleaned up the kitchen and started her prep work for their lunch. She loved the huge country kitchen and couldn't imagine ever getting bored working her magic in it.

Even more, she loved to cook for people who appreciated her food so much. It wasn't as much fun to prepare meals only for yourself and a toddler.

She was also well used to the men flirting with her. She knew it was lighthearted, but it was good for her ego. If any of them flirted a little beyond what she thought was appropriate, she quickly put them in their place and things went back to normal.

There was a new guy, though, one whom Mark had hired a couple of weeks after she'd started, who gave her the creeps. He never talked to her, but she would find him leering at her every once in a while. She was sure she just had an overactive imagination, but still, he never said a word to her, just let his eyes follow her wherever she went.

She would never consider saying anything to anyone about her fears. She was certain the new guy was harmless, like the rest of the men, and just trying to make a living. Still, her pep talks to herself didn't put an end to her uneasiness.

The guys returned for lunch in no time. Mark always looked so sexy in his dust-covered jeans and worn-out Stetson. It took every ounce of willpower not to stare at him, or pull him close.

"Hey, Emily, we're going over to the Three Rivers tonight. There's this great new singer who's performing. Do you want to come with us?" one of the hands asked her.

Emily was pleased to be invited, but she was worried about her son. Edward was in the kitchen and seemed to be able to read her mind. "I can keep an eye on the little man if you want to get out for a while," he offered.

"Are you sure?" she asked Edward.

"I'd love to watch him. We'll make some buttery popcorn and watch the new Disney movie," he said.

"Well, in that case, I'd love to," she said. She mentally went through her closet, excited to have a night out. It had been such a long time.

"I can give you a ride," John said.

"I'll bring Emily," Mark replied, brooking no argument from any of the men.

"I thought you said you couldn't make it, boss," John whined a little.

"I changed my mind," he said before throwing his hat back on and slamming out the back door.

"What burr's gotten under his saddle?" John grumbled.

"I think he's marking his territory," one of the other guys said.

"We're not a couple," Emily broke in. "He probably just didn't want to put any of you out."

"Sure," a few of the guys said in chorus. Everyone suddenly found great interest in their food, and no one else said a word as they finished their lunch and then dashed out the door.

Emily cleaned up quickly and hurried upstairs to get ready for her evening out. She had the whole afternoon to get ready, since everyone was going to eat dinner at the bar. She was actually a little giddy as she took a long bath and spent extra time on her hair, clothes, and makeup.

"Damn, girl, you look good. I call the first dance," said her favorite ranch hand, Eric, as she walked into the smoky bar with Mark. Her boss hadn't said one word to her on the ride there; he seemed to be angry with her, and she couldn't figure out why.

"Thank you, Eric, and yes, I'd love to dance with you," she told the man. He wasted no time in abandoning his seat and pulling her out onto the dance floor.

"So, it looks like the boss man is staking his claim," he said good-naturedly as he spun her in a circle.

"Don't be ridiculous, Eric. Things aren't like that between us. People have a bad day every once in a while," she said, not wanting rumors to start.

"If that's the case, then why are his eyes burning a hole in the back of my skull right now? I swear, he's about to leap up and attack me for having the nerve to dance with you. If I don't keep a respectable distance, I think he'll march over here and knock me out cold," he said with a chuckle.

"You are just being overly dramatic, as all you cowboys tend to be. Now, quit talking about Mark and focus on me. Isn't that what you're supposed to do when dancing with a lady?" she said with an amused huff.

"Yes, ma'am," he replied as he swung her in another circle. She liked Eric, just not enough to date him, which seemed to be the case with all the cowboys.

"My turn," Chris said as he approached.

"Aw, I was going for a second song," Eric complained.

"Tough," Chris told him as he pulled Emily into his arms, his arms wrapping around her, pulling her far closer than Eric had dared.

"It's your funeral," Eric murmured before clapping Chris on the back and laughing as he walked back to the table. This time, Emily could practically feel Mark's furious gaze on her, though she didn't understand it.

"I'm glad we finally got you out of the house," Chris said as he pressed his hips against hers. She was a little horrified when she thought she felt a slight bulge against her stomach. No. This wasn't what she wanted from him.

"I do like to escape the kitchen once in a while," she said as she tried to subtly pull back. He wasn't taking the hint, and she was a little upset now.

Looking over Chris's shoulder, she noticed the new ranch hand, David, peering at her, and the sudden feeling of being stalked was detracting from her happiness at having an evening out.

When the next song started, John came up and demanded his turn. Chris reluctantly released her with a promise to claim another dance.

"You sure look pretty tonight, Emily," John said with a blush. He held her respectfully.

"Well, you clean up mighty nice yourself, John. All this attention is going to go straight to my head, though," she said with a laugh.

"Aw, you're the prettiest girl in the room."

"I wouldn't be so sure of that, John. I see Misty over there at that table, and she can't seem to keep her eyes off you. I think you should ask her for the next dance."

John whipped his head around and then blushed again when he noticed the pretty redhead looking right at him. She quickly turned away and Emily was sure the girl's cheeks were hot, too.

"Maybe I should," he said eagerly.

"There's no *maybe* about it. You go and ask her as soon as this dance is over. I'd say go now, but you never leave your partner on the dance floor in the middle of a song," she said. "Your etiquette lesson for the day!"

"Thanks, Emily. You really are the best," he said with grateful eyes. She had the sudden urge to ruffle his hair, but didn't want to emasculate him. She found herself laughing through the song as John told her about a mean bull, then felt almost sad as the song came to a close.

"It's my turn to take this lady around the dance floor," said David, the creepy guy. He was standing too close to her and placed his hand on her back. She felt violated by just that little bit of touching.

She wished she could decline, but she was trapped because she hadn't turned any of the other guys down. He didn't put off good vibes at all. She closed her eyes and got ready to suffer through the dance.

"This dance is already taken," Mark said as he cut in.

Normally, Emily would have been irritated with any man who was as highhanded as Mark was being, but she was so relieved to be freed from dancing with David that she gladly accepted him as a partner.

Neither Mark nor Emily noticed the look David gave them both. He didn't say a word, but his hands clenched tight, and if looks could kill…

"You seem to be having a good time," Mark said through clenched teeth.

"I haven't been out in such a long while. I'm always just Mom, so, yes, I'm having a really great time. It's nice to hang out with adults," she said and then actually giggled as he spun her around.

The giggle stopped instantly when he slammed her body into his, pressing her close. He rubbed his hands from her shoulders, down her lower back, and up again. She felt electricity shooting from her stomach all the way to her toes.

"If you'd wanted to go out, all you had to do was say something," he snarled.

"Mark, why are you so upset? This is a fun night, and you should be enjoying yourself," she said to him, completely clueless.

"How do you expect me to enjoy myself when you're in the arms of other men? I've respected your wishes and haven't been pursuing you, but, dammit, I shouldn't have to watch you in the arms of my crew," he said, growing louder with each word he spoke.

He had her pulled so tightly against him she could barely breathe. She didn't even notice they'd stopped dancing. Luckily, the bar was loud and smoky, with a lot of people on the dance floor, and no one was paying them any attention.

Mark finally growled low in his throat and then crushed his lips down to hers. He pushed his tongue up against her bottom lip, demanding entrance, and she willingly obliged. She forgot all the reasons she'd decided that being with him was a bad idea and just enjoyed the moment in his arms.

His hands caressed her thighs, making the silk fabric that covered them draw up inch by inch. He was slowly walking the two of them into a dark corner where they could have more privacy. She couldn't even feel the movement of her own two feet. She was focused on nothing but Mark and what he was doing to her body.

His caressing fingers reached the edge of her dress and were stroking the uncovered top of her thighs that the garter belt was leaving exposed. She could feel the heat pooling in her core and she wanted him to relieve the pressure continuing to build there.

Her hands clutched tightly behind his neck, pulling him even closer. The kiss continued until she needed so much more from him than just his lips on hers. She needed him to join them together again. She needed it more than she needed air.

His lips left hers, allowing a gasp of air to enter, only to rush back out when he ran his tongue along the length of her throat. He nipped at her tender flesh, and she moaned in pleasure. "Please, Mark…" she begged.

"Uh, boss…" a voice interrupted them.

Emily slowly became aware of her surroundings again and realized they were practically making love up against a dirty wall in a bar. She was horrified at her own behavior. She had never been that kind of girl, brazen and shameless. She ducked her head into Mark's neck, hoping to avoid anyone's eyes.

"What do you want?" Mark snapped at the unfortunate guy.

"Um…the…the…bouncer over there said you guys need to break it up." The bearer of bad news was so embarrassed, he was stuttering.

Mark finally seemed to realize where he was and what he'd been doing and backed up a little bit from Emily. "Thanks," he mumbled to the poor kid. He then grabbed her hand and started pulling her toward the door.

"We are getting out of here now," he stated.

Emily had no desire to argue with him. She'd been fighting her own desires for too long, and it was time she got some satisfaction. "I'm ready to leave," she purred.

Mark walked out of the bar, not once letting go of her hand. When they reached his truck, he picked her up and sat her in the seat, slipping in between her opened legs. He pulled her close and kissed her deeply again. His hand slipped between their bodies, and he caressed her hardened nipple.

She heard a moan and was startled to realize the sound had come from her. "Please take me home," she begged him.

He kissed her one more time and then pushed her legs into the truck. He jumped in the driver's door and pulled out of the parking lot as if the place were about to explode. The drive back to the ranch took half the time it had taken to get to town. The silence was just as noticeable and fraught on the return trip, but for far different reasons.

They screeched to a stop a few feet from the front steps, and he leapt from the truck. "Please don't change your mind," he pleaded as he pulled open her door. Emily didn't answer him with words. She smiled seductively at him and then reached down and rubbed her hand over the bulging evidence of his desire as she leaned into him and ran her tongue over his neck.

"This is going to end too fast if you keep that up," he groaned. He then scooped her up into his arms and ran into the house and up the stairs. Emily didn't even know whether he got the front door closed.

He made it to the bedroom and then took her hard and fast against the door. Neither of them could hold out long enough to reach the bed.

Chapter Seventeen

Emily woke to find Mark staring down at her while rubbing her from the top of her thigh to her neck and back down. She could feel the desire start to pool again. How did he do that?

After their explosive lovemaking, they'd passed out in each other's arms on top of the covers. When the cool night air woke them, he'd made slow, sweet love to her again before they fell asleep, too exhausted to even move.

She glanced at the clock and was shocked to see it was almost noon. She'd slept for nine hours straight. She never did that. First, she'd almost gotten thrown out of a bar, and now… She groaned a bit as Mark's hand caressed her tender breasts and then teased her nipples.

"Mark, we need to talk…" she began.

"No," he said simply.

"Mark, listen…"

"No, this time, *you* listen," he said before pinning her hands above her head with one of his own as the other one continued caressing her body.

She wanted desperately to reason with him, but he was making it impossible to think. The feeling of being trapped beneath him and having him in complete control was extremely erotic. The hand that was touching her was causing her to lose all thoughts of stopping what they were doing.

"You will not run away this time. I understand all your reasons for wanting to keep things distant, but when two people have the kind of chemistry we have together, it's a crime not to pursue it. If it works out, great; if it doesn't, I promise I will take care of you," he said in between kissing her and nipping at her in places she hadn't known were sensitive until he touched them.

"You're making me sound like a mistress," she gasped while trying to remember why that was a bad thing.

"No, I want you as my girlfriend, my companion, my lover. I'd *never* try to buy you."

As he paused in his administering to show her how serious he was, she couldn't think of a single argument against what he was saying. She wanted him so much, and she really didn't see how they could go backward anyway.

"But what about Trevor?" she said in a last-ditch effort to speak rationally with him.

"I love Trevor," he said. "You must know that."

That was all it took for Emily to cave in. She couldn't fight him or the relationship anymore. He was still looking at her, waiting to see what she would say.

"Please kiss me," she finally pleaded. Her simple words were all it took to break the dam. They didn't leave the room for a few more hours.

When a guilt-ridden Emily finally made it downstairs and walked through the kitchen doors, Edward gave her a wink, which made her face turn a deep shade of red.

"How was your night?" he asked.

"It was great to get out," she mumbled. "I'm sorry I slept so long. Thank you for looking after Trevor."

"Trevor is a great kid," he replied. Trevor was sitting at the table, coloring, and hadn't noticed his mother's absence.

"How are you doing, love?" she asked as she walked over to kiss him on the head.

"Good, Mom. I got to stay up till after midnight," he said with awe.

"Wow, that's really late. You're simply getting too big."

"Mom, I'm *five*," he said. "I'm a big kid."

"I know. I just want you to stay my baby forever," she told him a little sadly.

"You can have another baby, and then I would be a big brother."

Emily was taken aback by the desire his statement caused inside her. She'd always wanted several children, but her ex had said one was more than enough. He'd never been the kind of father Trevor deserved, and to bring another kid into their lives would have been cruel to the unwanted baby.

"Maybe one day," she whispered wistfully.

"I can help you with that," Mark murmured in her ear as he entered the kitchen.

Emily turned an even darker shade of red and glanced at both Edward and Trevor to make sure they hadn't heard. They weren't paying any attention, thankfully, but his words put such a yearning in her heart that she felt an ache there and unconsciously rubbed at her chest.

She didn't see the dark desire in Mark's eyes. He might have been goading her, but he was incredibly surprised to realize he would be ecstatic if she were to become pregnant. That thought was enough to knock him speechless.

Emily was turned sideways, so he glanced down at her flat stomach, imagining it blooming outward as his child grew there. The desire was so intense, he could barely breathe. He was going to make sure she didn't ever leave his life. He didn't know how this woman had so quickly crawled into his heart, but she was there, and he had no desire — zero — to let her leave.

"I need to go tend the horses," he suddenly said and practically ran out the door.

Emily breathed a sigh of relief. She didn't know how she was supposed to act around him. She didn't know whether he wanted Edward to know they were a couple. She didn't know anything.

But why get stressed out about it? Surely they had time to work it all out.

*****

Emily felt as if someone was following her. She kept looking back, but the eerie feeling wouldn't go away. Trevor was at school, and Mark was working somewhere on the ranch, so she'd wanted to get some fresh air. Now that she was a couple of miles away from the house and felt that someone was stalking her, she knew it hadn't been such a good idea.

Just calm down, she told herself. *You're just letting your overheated imagination get to you. Everything is fine.* Even so, she picked up her pace a bit as she moved toward the safety of the house.

When she heard a shuffling in the bushes, not far from where she was, a little squeal escaped her lips, and she began to jog. She looked over her shoulder the entire way back and breathed a huge sigh of relief when she saw the barn come into view, but she still couldn't shake the spooky feeling.

"Where have you been?"

Emily's heart jumped into her throat as a light scream escaped her lips. She whipped around to see Mark astride his huge horse, eyeing her with concern.

"Calm down, boy," Mark soothed his animal. He gave her another searching look.

"Sorry, Mark, you startled me," she said, completely out of breath.

"I can see that. Are you OK?" he asked as he jumped down from his horse and walked over to her slowly, as if she were a scared animal.

"I'm fine. I just spooked myself out on my walk. I got too far from the house and started picturing evil forces following me," she said with a laugh. Now that she was back in the safety of the ranch, she realized how silly she had been.

"Were you out that way?" she asked him while pointing in the direction she'd just come from.

"No, I just came in from the east fields," he replied and looked questioningly out into the woods she had come from. "Did you see something?"

"No, it was nothing like that. I'm sure some squirrels were playing around in the bushes. I seriously have got to stop reading all those Stephen King novels," she said sheepishly.

"I agree. You do tend to jump at the smallest sound."

"Well, you didn't have to agree so quickly," she huffed, her fear evaporating as indignation took its place.

"Come with me; I want to show you something," he said, ignoring her mild outburst and taking her hand. He led his horse with the other one.

"Do you never get enough?" she teased him.

He pulled her into his arms and kissed her gently before reluctantly releasing her and heading toward the smaller of the barns. "Baby, I never get enough of you, but that's not what I want to show you," he answered with a gleam in his eyes.

They fell into a comfortable silence as they strolled toward the barn. Mark handed his horse off to one of the men and then led her to the loft. Inside a hole in the hay lay a mama kitty and five brand new kittens. They were crawling all over her, looking for food.

"Oh, Mark, they're adorable," she cried and sat down to pet the mama. The cat purred and leaned her head into the rub. "I can't wait to show Trevor,"

Emily added as she gently ran her finger down the little orange one's head.

The mama got tired of being used for only her milk and sauntered off, leaving the kittens crying out.

"Will they be OK?" Emily asked.

"Of course they will. She just went off to get some food. She won't leave them long," he said gently.

"Can I hold one?" she asked him hopefully.

"Sure."

She carefully picked up the adorable little orange kitten and cuddled it to her breast. It rooted around for a moment and, when it came up empty, let out a frustrated cry, then quickly fell asleep. Emily didn't know how long she sat there cuddling the new kitten, but its mother soon returned, so she reluctantly laid the baby back down to nurse.

"Are you keeping them?" she asked hopefully, trying to come off as nonchalant, but failing miserably.

"Do you want to keep them?" he asked.

"It's up to you," she stalled.

"You're so stubborn. Just admit you want to keep the kittens." He exhaled as he combed through his untamed hair with his hand.

"Fine. I want them to stay," she mumbled and folded her arms across her chest. She knew it was irrational to be so against asking for even the smallest thing, but the more Mark did for her and Trevor, the more she was afraid of losing it all. She was already impossibly attached. The kittens were just one more attachment that was linking her to the ranch.

"Now, was that so hard?" he asked.

She realized she was being silly, but she didn't know how else to protect herself. They'd been making love nightly for almost a month, and he treated Trevor like a son. She was afraid everything was too perfect and her bubble was going to break at any moment.

"We like to have a lot of cats around. They keep the mice and rats away," he told her.

"Rats are so much bigger than they are," she exclaimed, looking around in case a huge rat came to pounce on the innocent kittens at any moment.

"I think the other cats will take care of the rodents until these guys grow up a bit more," he said with a chuckle.

Mark left her with the kittens while he finished his chores. She had no idea how much time had passed until Trevor suddenly raced into the barn.

"Mom, Mark said you have a surprise to show me," her son said, trying to gain his breath as he placed his head between his legs.

"Come over here, and don't be loud," she whispered.

Trevor's eyes got big as he walked over to his mom, and then he squealed when he saw the babies. "Are they all ours?" he asked with excitement.

"Yep, Mark said we get to keep them all," she told him.

"Cool! Can I hold one?"

"Sure you can. But you have to be really gentle and pet their mama for a few minutes first."

Trevor obediently gave attention to the adult cat and then gently held the tiger-striped one. They stayed there for a while longer, and then Emily had to head up to the house to get dinner ready.

"Can I stay out here with Mark, please?" Trevor pleaded. Emily looked down to where Mark was, and he nodded his head yes.

"OK, but be good, and when Mark tells you it's time to come in, no fussing," she told him.

"Of course, Mom," he said.

Chapter Eighteen

It wasn't one strange thing; it was several. Nothing by itself was particularly alarming, but when she added it all up, Emily was starting to creep herself out.

First there were the flowers. She'd received a dozen red roses with a card signed "From a Secret Admirer." She'd thought it was Mark trying to be cute, until he asked her where they had come from. When she showed him the note, he laughed it off and told her it was probably John, the young ranch hand who had a slight crush on her. She thought that might be right and didn't want to embarrass the kid, so she displayed the roses on the kitchen table and thought nothing else about them.

Then, over the next few weeks, in the mailbox at the end of the road, she found little notes saying she was beautiful and smart. None of the notes was harmful in the least, and she still wasn't concerned, but at the same time she also had the feeling someone was secretly watching her. When she put everything together, it was enough to make her start thinking something was seriously wrong.

She thought the flowers could have come from John, but not the notes. She knew he had a slight crush, but he wasn't the type to be a stalker. Plus, the eerie feeling of being watched would come over her when she knew for a fact that John was nowhere near the house. She thought some of it could be the creepy ranch hand, David, but again, things were happening when she knew he was far from the house with Mark.

She figured she was just overreacting and kept all the little incidents to herself. She didn't want to concern Mark with any of it. Feeling a little freaked out wasn't a reason to call in the National Guard. She attributed it to her overactive imagination and decided to take a few more safety precautions.

The next day though, when Emily went to check the mail and found an envelope in the box addressed to her, everything changed. There was no return address on it, but it had been mailed locally. She opened it, not thinking much about it until she read the words.

I have been watching you. I love how your hair blows in the breeze when you step out onto the balcony late at night. You are truly a vision. I know you've noticed me as well but have to keep up appearances. I just wanted to let you know that I'm here for you and will always be here. We were meant to be together. Nothing will keep us apart. I know you'll enjoy what I have planned for

us. It will be magical. Until we're together, know I'm keeping an eye on you. I hope you've appreciated my poetry and the gifts I have left for you. Just know if I can't have you, then no one else can either. We will be a true family soon.
With all my love,
Yours forever

Emily dropped the letter and started shaking uncontrollably. She looked around the place, fearful there was someone watching her at that moment. A shiver of fear ran down her spine, and tears filled her eyes. She was terrified to know her fears had been real.

Who would do something like this — who would try to scare another person? Was the person actually trying to frighten her, or was he insane? Did it matter? No.

If someone was out to get her, then she was putting her son and everyone else in the home in danger. She couldn't allow that to happen. She couldn't let the people she loved come to harm because a crazy person was intent on getting her.

Suddenly all those times she'd felt eyes on her came to the fore, and terror seized her. How close had this person come to her? Why must this happen when she was finally feeling secure for the first time since she'd escaped her former in-laws?

Her emotion overflowed and Emily fell to the floor and sobbed. She'd known that things were too good to be true. Pain ripped through her very soul at the thought of having to leave, but how could she stay and jeopardize those she cared most about?

Mark walked in the front door, and his heart nearly stopped when he saw Emily huddled on the floor with sobs racking her body. He dropped to his knees and gathered her into his arms. Never before had he seen her like this, looking utterly broken.

"Emily, what's happened? Is Trevor OK?" he asked in a panic. He gently shook her shoulders so she would look at him. He needed to know what was wrong so he could fix it. There wasn't any doubt in his mind that he would indeed be able to handle whatever the problem was.

She glanced up at him with haunted eyes. She looked terrified, and he knew he would go to the ends of the world to fight whatever demons were after her. He gathered her close while the sobs continued unabated. His eyes sought frantically for Trevor. He could deal with anything else that was happening if he knew Trevor was OK.

Edward walked into the room and immediately rushed over. "What on earth has happened?" he asked.

"I don't know," Mark answered. "Is Trevor OK?"

"Yes, Trevor is fine," Edward said. "He's in the kitchen."

Mark visibly relaxed. "Can you go stay with Trevor and make sure he doesn't come in? I'm going to take Emily up to our room and find out what is going on."

"Of course, sir," Edward replied. His eyes followed the two as Mark gently carried Emily up the stairs. He was as concerned about her as Mark was, for Emily had already become a loved member of the household.

Mark laid her on the bed and then stretched out next to her, holding her until the sobs finally started to quiet down. When she was down to just a few hiccups, he pleaded with her to tell him what was going on.

"W…we are g…going to have to m…move," she finally managed to get out between sobs.

Mark felt as if his whole world had been flipped upside down. "Why would you even think that?" he asked.

"Trevor isn't safe," she managed to gasp out and then handed him the letter that was crushed in her hand.

Mark read it through and then read it again to make sure he was really seeing what was there. He still held her close and made sure to gently rub her back, but if she had been able to see his eyes, her terror would have tripled.

He was simmering with so much fury, it took all the well-trained willpower he'd ever developed not to smash up the room. He knew he had to stay calm and strong for her, but how dare someone try to threaten his woman?

He'd always heard people talk about seeing red when they lost their temper, and he had thought it was nothing more than an expression. He now understood the reality of it. His fury was so intense, he could actually see a red hue around the corners of his vision.

"It's OK, baby; I promise you this person will never come near you or Trevor," he said with so much menace in his tone that she actually stopped crying long enough to look up at him in surprise.

He didn't want her to see his eyes, so he gently tucked her head back down to his shoulder while he continued stroking her.

"You don't understand, Mark; he knows where I live. He could hurt Trevor while trying to get to me," she said. The tears were finally starting to dry.

"Emily, I will repeat to you that I'll never let anything happen to you or Trevor. I guarantee this guy won't touch you," he stated. He lifted her chin up, looking deeply into her eyes. He'd finally managed to gain some control over his turbulent emotions.

"How can you promise me that?"

"I was raised always to protect those I love," he simply stated.

Emily inhaled deeply as she realized what he'd said. She didn't think he even realized he'd said he loved her. Her heart filled with so much warmth and light, and it was beginning to vanquish the total devastation that was beating from within her chest.

"You're a good man, Mark, too good a man. I keep waiting to find a fault in you, and I can't find a single one. How did I get so lucky as to meet you?" She was honestly puzzled.

"Oh, Emily, I'm the lucky one. I may not have been looking for a relationship, but with you in my life, I can't remember what it was like not having you by my side. I could never let harm come to you or Trevor. I'm sure this is nothing, that someone just thinks they are being funny. Don't let it worry you.

Trevor is always watched, and my men will stay close to the house until we figure this out."

With the soothing feel of his hands caressing her, and his gentle words reassuring her, Emily snuggled more deeply into Mark's strong arms and fell asleep, exhausted by all the turmoil that had been in her heart.

Once Mark knew Emily was sleeping, he got up and made a few phone calls. The first one was to an old high school friend who was a classified military intelligence agent. If anyone could get answers about who was stalking Emily, it was Chad.

"It's been a while," Chad said in place of a greeting.

"That's because I never know when you will answer," Mark replied.

"I will always answer for you — even in the middle of a gunfight," Chad said. He was laughing, though Mark was a bit worried his friend might have been speaking the truth.

"Can you come help me out?" There was no point in beating around the bush.

"Of course. Give me a couple of days to get there."

Chad asked no questions about why he was needed; that was just who he was. He had honor and would do anything for those he cared about. The thought of ever becoming his enemy, on the other hand, made Mark shiver. No one would want to be on Chad's bad side.

Mark took a moment and explained the situation, and Chad promised to find out what was going on, swearing that the letter writer would never harm either Emily or Trevor. Mark smiled at the tone in his friend's voice. He knew he'd made the right choice in calling him.

The next call was to his father. Joseph listened as Mark read the letter. "I'll be right over. And I'll call your brothers" was all he said before hanging up the phone.

Mark went back to the bedroom to lie next to Emily. He didn't want her to wake up alone and panic. He needed to be there for her, to reassure her that everything was going to be OK.

Chapter Nineteen

Emily woke in Mark's arms and for a moment forgot all about the letter and the devastation it had brought to her peace of mind. He was pressed up against her back, and his desire for her was obvious. She rubbed against him, automatically stretching and pressing her backside closer to his hardness.

"You simply take my breath away. I can barely breathe," Mark mumbled into her hair as he kissed her neck and ran his hand gently up her side to cup her ample breast. The peak hardened instantly at his touch and she pressed herself into him, trying to get as close as possible.

"That's the plan," she purred.

He slowly turned her, and they made love with a sweetness that was beyond anything she'd ever felt before. She was really starting to feel loved by this wonderful man; she still couldn't believe he was a part of her life.

"I would much prefer to stay here in bed with you all day, but we have guests," he said as he nibbled on her neck some more.

Suddenly, the hours before she'd passed out came flooding back, and Emily's whole body stiffened. She was saddened to be brought back so suddenly to reality.

"It's OK, baby; I called my family, and they are here so we can all come up with a game plan. We're a family, and we protect each other."

"You shouldn't have bothered them with this. I'm not their concern," she said, perplexed.

Mark stared at her as if she'd lost her mind. "Do you really think either you or Trevor are any less important than I am?" he asked her incredulously.

"I just meant that your family didn't have to drop everything because I got some creepy letter," she tried to explain.

"That letter should be taken seriously, and we're going to make sure you're safe," he told her with finality. He was acutely aware that letters like that could lead to grave danger. He might have tried to downplay it to her so she could sleep, but when you grew up as wealthy as he had, threats were never taken lightly. If she'd known how frightened he really was, she wouldn't have been able to leave the safety of their bed.

Emily shrugged, caving in to his demands. "I'm going to shower really quickly before heading down."

"Do you need someone to scrub your back?" he asked with a wink.

"Then neither of us would ever get down there," she said. She gave him a quick kiss and then firmly shut the bathroom door behind her.

Mark lay on the bed thinking of each moment he spent with her. He loved her strong will, and he loved her kindness. He was falling in love with her. It scared the hell out of him, but at the same time, it felt right. He saw no need to fight it.

He finally made his way downstairs and was surprised to see his entire family. Not only had his dad come with his brothers, but they had brought their spouses and children, too.

"Uncle Mark!" Jasmine yelled and threw her arms around his legs. "You took forever to come down. Daddy said you were *comforting* Aunt Emily," she said and put quotation marks around the word *comforting,* just as her daddy had done. She had no idea what she was saying, but Mark glared at his brother anyway.

"Isn't my niece a little bit young for you to be corrupting?" Mark asked Lucas.

"Hey, I was just telling her what a good comforter you are," Lucas goaded him.

"Quit your fighting; we have things to discuss and people to beat the shit out of," Alex said.

"Language, Alex," Jessica scolded.

"Sorry, honey," Alex said sheepishly.

"I called Chad. He'll be here in a couple days. I'm not sure where he's flying from, but it must be far," Mark informed them.

"I'm glad to hear he's coming in to help out," Joseph said with relief evident in his voice.

"Me, too," Mark said. He was already feeling better about Emily's safety with just his family in the room. There was no way anyone would get to her with his brothers there.

"We're staying here until this gets solved," Lucas said. The rest of the people in the room all nodded their heads in agreement.

"I've already prepared the rooms," Edward remarked as he set out beverages and snacks.

Mark blinked several times as his eyes began to sting. He couldn't imagine life without his family. He truly felt sorry for those millions of people who didn't have the same support system.

He was grateful he had more money than most, but he would give up every last dime before he would give up one member of his family. He realized that included Emily and Trevor as well.

Mark poured himself a double shot of whiskey and enjoyed the burning sensation as it slid down his throat and burned its way to his gut.

"Thank you, guys; we'll get this solved immediately," he said to everyone.

Emily walked into the room just then, and her eyes widened at the large crowd before her. She didn't have time to say anything, though, because Jessica and Amy ran up to her and wrapped her in a group hug.

"We're so sorry someone is doing this," Amy said.

"We'll never let anything happen to you," Jessica added.

The three women stood together. They wiped a few tears and then quickly laughed, feeling secure as a unit. They'd already formed a bond stronger than most sisters. The guys crept back from them as if they were contagious. They didn't know how to deal with feminine emotions.

"Women," Alex whispered.

"Yeah, I know," Lucas said.

"I don't get them," Mark added.

"Seriously, guys kill the problem while girls are always crying, but that's why we have to be there to protect them," Joseph piped in. It was a good thing their wives didn't hear their comments.

All four men nodded their heads in unison while heading to the barn to start discussing safety measures on the property. They didn't have a clue one person was watching them the entire time. One person Mark would never have even considered suspecting.

Chapter Twenty

"Good, the men are gone. Now, you can tell us everything," Amy said as the three women sat down in the living room and accepted drinks from Edward before he quietly left them to speak alone.

"Now that I've had time to rest, I really don't think it's that big a deal," Emily told them, unwilling to make something out of nothing.

"Don't give us that, Emily. Mark was seriously freaked out. Lucas and Alex were planning on storming up here and kicking some major ass, and both Jessica and I insisted on coming along. We knew something wasn't right."

"I don't know…" Emily still hedged. If something was seriously wrong, she didn't want it to be, not with Jessica and Amy there, and the kids, as well. Too many people were now involved. It scared her more than the letter had.

"I can sit here all night. How about you, Jessica?"

"Yep. I have nowhere else to be."

Emily looked at her two friends and knew they were serious. She was either speaking or they weren't letting her leave. She smiled gratefully at them.

"It started a couple of months ago. I had the feeling that I was being watched. I shrugged it off, thinking I had to be going insane. There are men all over the place here. Of course, someone probably had their eye on me. It's just that I kept getting this feeling like it was something serious."

"Yeah, like women's intuition. You should have spoken up then," Jessica said, her eyes wide.

"No. I would have looked foolish. Besides, I never actually *saw* anyone. I just had a feeling. Then I got flowers and all these love notes, and I thought maybe it was John, a really nice ranch hand, thinking he was being cute. I didn't want to hurt his feelings, so again I ignored the warnings."

"With the feeling of being watched and the notes, you should have done something," Amy told her sternly.

"It wasn't anything to fret about. Seriously," she said when both women narrowed their eyes at her.

"Keep talking," Amy said.

"Today I got this," she said as she handed the women the note.

They both read over it slowly, probably several times since neither spoke for several moments. When Amy looked up, her eyes were wide and she looked worried.

"We got here just in time. This isn't just some crush, Emily. This is something a lot more frightening than that. This man means business, and it looks like he's letting you know that he's not happy to remain on the sidelines anymore."

"That's how I felt about it, Jessica. It's just that I don't know what to do. I don't want Mark putting himself in danger, or Lucas or Alex. I told him that Trevor and I could leave —"

"That's nonsense. Do you honestly think Mark would ever let that happen? Do you find him that weak that he can't protect his woman?"

Emily shook her head. No. Mark was the strongest man she knew. He was kind and gentle and giving and the exact opposite of her deceased husband.

"No, of course not. He's your guy. Let him take care of you. Well, let him think he's taking care of you. Jessica and I are really the ones who will be doing it," Amy said with a smile as she leaned in and gave Emily a hug.

"You both mean so very much to me. Thank you for caring," Emily said, her voice choking up.

When she'd found that job listing in the paper, she hadn't ever imagined finding a whole new family. Losing her parents had been devastating. Being an only child and having no one to turn to after the loss was even worse. Now, if she lost this family, which was bound to happen eventually, she'd go through a whole new mourning period.

"I hate that you came out here and there's even a fraction of a chance that you can get hurt, but at the same time, I'm so very glad you're here," Emily told them.

"We are too, Emily. You're our sister now, and we protect our family. Even Katie is here to help," she said with a wink.

Katie was sleeping peacefully in her portable bassinet at the moment, but Emily couldn't wait for her to wake so she could cuddle her close. There was something about holding a baby that took a person's fears all away. Maybe it was their pureness or their untouched soul. Whatever it was, having a baby in the house was special.

"She *is* an Anderson. I think she could take the stalker," Jessica said with a smile.

"I think you may be right. When those three brothers are together, I'd certainly cross the street if they were gunning for me," Emily said with a giggle.

"Well, you want to know something else?" Amy said with a smile.

"What?" both Emily and Jessica asked.

"Katherine was going through old albums with me since I love to scrapbook so much, and I ran across a family picture from about six years ago. If you think the three boys are hot, you should see a photo of them with their cousins!"

"I haven't heard of any cousins," Emily said, trying to remember all the photos she'd seen in the house.

"I don't know the whole story, but they have four cousins, three of whom are incredibly sexy males. You can certainly see the family resemblance. I guess their mom died four years ago, and they kind of fell apart. It's tragic."

"Oh, that's awful. I can't imagine the Anderson men ever letting a family member leave. They are so loyal," Emily said.

"I know. It goes back a long time. Joseph and George had a feud, and then parted ways, his brother moving to Chicago. They did make up, but George stayed over there, with the family just visiting back and forth. Then when his wife died, he was so devastated that he took off and hasn't spoken to anyone since. It rips Joseph apart. According to Katherine, though, Joseph is done with George's being away. He's planning on hunting his brother down. He told his wife that in times of crisis family needs each other even more."

"Now that I can picture Joseph saying," Jessica said. "I vaguely remember the cousins, but I was so dang shy way back then that I didn't come around if the family had visitors. Three sexy men in addition to Lucas, Alex and Mark — that would have sent me scurrying for the hills," she said with a giggle.

"I'm with you," Emily and Amy agreed, which made all three women laugh.

"What do you ladies find so amusing?" Joseph asked as he stepped into the room.

"About how arrogant your sons are," Amy said with a cheeky grin.

"Ah, that they are, lassie, that they are," he said as he went to the liquor cabinet and poured himself a shot of bourbon.

"Did the boys kick you out?" Jessica asked.

"Not at all, dear. I would just much rather spend my time in the presence of lovely ladies," he said with a wink.

Emily knew he was talking to his daughters-in-law, but she still found herself blushing, and she looked down. She would enjoy being included in his family, more than she'd ever care to admit.

"I'm sure happy to see you smiling. A family is strong when they're together. You three stick together now," Joseph said as he leaned back and closed his eyes.

"We will," Jessica said as she and Amy linked their arms through Emily's.

Emily was so full of emotion, she couldn't speak for several moments, and was grateful when they moved on to lighter topics. By the time she went to bed that night in Mark's arms, her worries were pushed so far beneath the surface, she had no trouble falling asleep.

She hated to admit it, but having her own personal knight was pretty spectacular.

Chapter Twenty-One

Two days of nothing — shouldn't that have felt better? But waiting never does.

No one let Emily get out of sight. She was grateful, to be sure, but she was also beginning to feel a bit claustrophobic. She'd been staying almost nightly in Mark's room already, so while they had visitors, he moved her things in there, making their sleeping arrangements more permanent.

Mark explained it was safer for her to stay with him, and with all the extra houseguests, they needed her room anyway. She was afraid it would affect Trevor, but he didn't seem to notice anything unusual about the situation.

Mark and Emily made love each night, and her worry seemed to fade away into nothingness. She knew beyond a shadow of a doubt she was in love with Mark, and if he were to grow bored with her, she didn't know what she would do. She was in the very situation she'd tried so hard to avoid.

But how could she not love him when he was so caring to and about her and treated her son as if he were his own? The rest of his family also treated her and Trevor as if they were a part of their family. She'd choked up the first time Jasmine called her Aunty Emily, but now she was starting to get used to it. She found she really liked the way it sounded.

She was sitting out on the back deck when the most incredibly built guy she'd ever come in contact with stepped up next to her. With his short dark hair and aviator glasses, he could easily be stepping off the set of a spy movie. She would bet money that women would melt from just a wink from him. Curiosity had her wanting to ask him to remove his glasses.

She should be terrified of this stranger, but she had no doubt this was Chad, the buddy whom Mark had been talking about.

"Chad, you made it!" Mark exclaimed as he came around the corner.

"Sorry I couldn't get here sooner," Chad replied.

Damn! Even the sound of his voice was like a cup of warm apple cider on a crisp fall morning. She decided they had to be putting something special in the food in that area, because all the men seemed to be too sexy for any normal person's good.

"This is my Emily," Mark said as they came up to her.

Emily felt her heart swell as he called her his. Mark never tried to hide the way he was feeling from her, but it was still amazingly gratifying to have him behave so possessively. She wanted to be his, enjoyed them being a couple.

"It's a pleasure to meet you, Emily. I wish it were under better circumstances." He held out his hand and for the briefest moment, Emily didn't know what to do. Finally, her brain kicked in and she stood up, giving him her hand.

"Thank you for coming, Chad. I'm sure all the fuss is over nothing, but if it brought Mark's friend here, then it is all worth it," she said with a smile.

He pulled his glasses off, and she smiled. Yep. She'd been right about the eyes. They were piercing and blue, and would make a sinner lie down and confess. Mark had said he was single, and she didn't know how the heck that was possible.

Maybe he had some weird fetishes or he was a control freak. Who knew? Emily knew one thing for sure, though — there were a lot of women out there who just wouldn't care how he acted. He was that heart-stoppingly gorgeous.

A bit of guilt consumed her at thinking such thoughts about another man. It wasn't that she wanted him; it was just that she was a young woman and could appreciate true beauty in a man. As long as the interest was purely aesthetic, what was sauce for the gander… She'd have bet her life that when he and Mark had walked side by side in school, they'd ruled the hallways. She'd love to hear some of those stories.

"Follow me," Mark told him, and started walking into the house.

"I look forward to talking to you later," Chad said to Emily before turning and going after Mark

"If I weren't head over heels in love with my husband, I think I would jump up on that man and beg him to take me to paradise," Amy said as she moved beside Emily.

"I was thinking the same thing. Where has Mark been hiding him?" Jessica said with a giggle.

Emily was shocked at first, but since she was thinking the same thoughts, it suddenly cracked her up and she started laughing so hard, she couldn't breathe. When she finally caught her breath she looked at the two women with merriment.

"Where do these guys come from? Really? Are we secretly being filmed? It should honestly be criminal to have that good of looks, all this money, and such incredible sexual prowess."

"Um, how do you know about Chad's sexual prowess?" Amy asked with a laugh.

"Oh, I was talking about Mark's, but believe me, I am sure Chad could rattle the shingles off some roofs."

Both women looked at her with stunned gazes before they joined her in laughter.

"Oh Emily, you were so meant to be our sister," Jessica said. "It's time for some spiked tea. I'm all hot and bothered, suddenly."

The women walked around to the pool and continued their quipping.

"I swear if all of them walk out here shirtless right now, I will not be responsible for my actions," Amy announced.

"Ditto. I'm so ready to take my husband, my toes are tingling," Jessica said.

Emily had a few thoughts on what she'd like to be doing with Mark, and she smiled as she laid her head back and imagined it in detail.

*****

"OK, Chad, I want the guys to think you're a new hire. Luckily, you've been out of the country long enough that only my foreman knows who you are. I already filled him in on what's happening, so he won't say a word. You're going to get more information if the guys think you're one of them. I'm sorry; you'll have to sleep in the bunkhouse," he added with an evil grin.

"Yeah, you look sorry about that," Chad said. "Good thing I've slept in much worse places."

"Yeah, I kind of wish it were a little rougher out there," Mark continued.

"You're a peach. I'd better get changed. I want to check things out right away. The sooner we make sure your Emily is safe, the sooner everyone can relax."

"I appreciate the way you dropped everything to do this. She's the one, Chad. I've never felt this way about another woman," Mark admitted to his friend.

"I knew that the second we spoke on the phone," Chad told him before heading off to change into some less conspicuous clothing. He was going to have a hard enough time blending in with his size and demeanor, but add the clothes he was currently wearing, and the man looked like the military badass that he was.

Chad changed quickly and headed down to the bunkhouses where the ranch foreman was. Without conscious thought, he was alert to everything around him. He noticed the men working on the fence off to his right and the guy to his left feeding the horses. He wasn't an easy man to sneak around. He would catch this stalker in a matter of days, if not hours.

Chad wasn't a cocky man; he was just incredibly confident. He'd been in the military for almost twenty years, and those years had taught him well. There were few people in his life he would drop everything for. Mark happened to be one of those select few.

If it hadn't been for Mark and his family, Chad's life would have turned out significantly different. They had believed in him and helped him get out of the horrible circumstances he'd been in to make a success out of his life.

Chad shook off the distracting thoughts and stepped through the bunkhouse doors. He spotted the foreman right away, sitting down at a table along with a couple of the other ranch hands. He walked up to the men with his usual confidence and introduced himself.

"Morning; I'm Chad. Mark hired me and said to come down here and get set up," Chad said while sticking out his hand.

The men eyed him warily, as if sizing up a new bull. The foreman finally stood and Chad was impressed with the man's acting skills. A normal observer would never have known they were already acquainted.

"Good to meet you, Chad. I'm Bob, the foreman here," he said and clasped his hand.

"Good to meet you as well."

"Why don't you get settled in today and get the lay of the land? You can begin work tomorrow," Bob said, giving Chad the time he needed in order to scope out the area and do some snooping through the hands' things.

Once the other men headed back out to do their work, Chad and Bob sat down and discussed the operation. Chad wanted to know what was normal behavior for the men, whether anyone had raised Bob's suspicions, and if anything seemed out of the ordinary to him.

Bob promised to keep the men away from the bunkhouse between three and five, which would give Chad plenty of time to search it. For now, Chad headed out to survey the grounds.

He didn't see anything suspicious right off, but he didn't have much time and would have to do a more thorough search the next day. He really wanted to go through the hands' rooms. He was far more likely to find fishy items there.

This had to be an inside job — they almost always were.

At three on the dot, he slipped back into the bunkhouse without anyone seeing him and began searching through the men's belongings.

*****

"It's time to get out of here for a while. The guys can take care of the kids. I'm in desperate need of a pedicure," Jessica said to Emily and Amy.

"Ooh, great thinking, Jess. I'll let Lucas know and be ready to leave in twenty minutes. I just want to change," Amy said and then dashed off to her room.

"That does sound nice. I hate to leave Trevor with everything going on, though," Emily said.

"He'll be fine. No one can get through our men," Jessica assured her.

Emily really loved to think of Mark as her man. She wasn't exactly sure where they stood, but so far, things seemed to be just about as perfect as they could get. Well, as perfect as it could be while she was being stalked by some unknown psycho.

"You're right, of course. I'll go change and be down quickly," Emily said and ran upstairs.

"Be careful, and don't stay gone too long," Mark said to Emily. He knew he would be worried about her while she was out. He also knew she needed some time away from the house. Her nerves were fried. The girls would be able to get her mind off of her worries, and she would get to relax, something that would help more than anything else.

"Try not to max out the charge cards," Lucas teased them.

"I'm sorry, but we can't make any promises," Amy told her husband with a wink. Lucas smiled as they headed out the doors. Amy was so much more confident than the woman he'd met years ago. She was still frugal, but she finally felt like an equal in the marriage. He'd drummed into her head that money was nothing without love, and that what was his was hers, and she finally felt she could go out with the girls without having to justify every little purchase. He was gratified to see her unbend.

"I love that woman," Lucas said as the three women disappeared down the driveway.

"Ditto, Brother," Alex said.

"I'm right there with you," Mark added.

Both brothers turned to smile at Mark. They were happy he seemed to have found the one. The fact she came with an instant family was an added bonus. It showed how much the three men had grown that they didn't even try to tease Mark.

"I can't believe how hard we all fought to hold on to our bachelorhood. What the hell were we thinking?" Alex asked.

"Seriously," Lucas agreed. "I was bad, but, Alex, you were a moron," he added.

"I know. I hate even thinking about what I put Jessica through. She never brings it up, never tries to load me with guilt me for the pain I caused. I still don't deserve her, but I try to make it up to her every single day. I would fall on a knife for that woman!"

"That's what love does to you. It makes you want to write poems, and buy flowers. It makes you want to fall down at their feet. Never, ever, and I mean *ever*, tell the guys at the office that I said any of this," Lucas warned.

"I'm with you. They'd think we'd gone soft and all sorts of chaos would ensue," Alex agreed.

"I thought falling in love with just one woman would be the end of me, but watching you guys with your wives and seeing how happy they've made you over the years has really put a craving in me for something more. I've felt like there was something missing. I was still determined not to get married, but since Emily has walked into my life, I can't seem to think of anything else," Mark said.

"Does that mean you're going to pop the question?" Lucas asked in surprise. His little brother had been with Emily for only a few months. Wasn't it too soon?

"Yes, but not yet. It's way too soon for marriage, but I just know that I can't ever let her go. On top of that, I really love Trevor. I want him to be my son. His father is gone, and from what I've found out, his father's parents are terrible people. Emily's parents are gone, too."

"What do you know of his terrible grandparents?" Alex asked.

"Emily hasn't opened up to me yet, but I wanted to find out what she was so frightened of when she first got here. It was pretty obvious that she was hiding from something. I just needed to make sure it wasn't something too serious."

"Is it something that can be fixed?" Lucas asked, always wanting to be the hero.

"I don't know the full story, because I refuse to snoop too far into her life. I just know that her marriage wasn't a good one, that her ex didn't treat her or Trevor well. I also know that his parents were even worse to her."

"Why don't you find out more? What if it's something serious?" Lucas didn't like answers left unanswered.

"She will come to me, Lucas. I need to give her time."

"Well, if you're OK with that, I guess we have to be, too," Alex said, but neither of his brothers were happy with waiting. If something needed fixing, they wanted to do it right then.

"I appreciate that you both have my back," Mark said feelingly.

"All right, we have got to change this subject. I'm going to stress all night if I don't get a drink and watch a game. I don't want Amy to know, but I don't like the way this is all so unanswered, and it worries me to have her out while it's going on."

"Yeah, I feel the same, but they are safer away from the house than here. We're safe too — as long as they don't find out we have a guard following them."

"Crap, that wouldn't go over at all well," Lucas said.

"Dad has sure been acting smug about seeing us all settling down," Alex said with a laugh.

"Yeah, he pushed us for a long time," Mark said.

"At least we found our own women without his meddling," Lucas said.

The three men laughed at what they perceived as their independence. Joseph happened to be around the corner and overheard his three sons talking. He was getting his own laughs in at their sad delusions. Someday, he would tell them the truth. No, as he thought of what Katherine's reaction would be, he thought maybe he wouldn't after all. But at least he would be able to pat himself on the back.

Chapter Twenty-Two

"Oh, my gosh; this feels so good," Emily exclaimed as a woman rubbed lightly scented lotion into her feet.

"Seriously, I think I have died and gone to heaven," Amy purred. Her feet were sitting in the hot, bubbly scented water.

"I'm never leaving," Jessica added as her toenails were being painted a deep shade of red.

The three girls were being tended to in luxuriously comfortable chairs and talking about anything and everything.

"I love being a mother, but it's so nice to get away and have some time with my two best friends," Amy said.

"Agreed," Jessica and Emily said in unison.

After they finished with their pedicures and manicures, they walked through the huge Seattle mall. "I'm in need of some sexy lingerie," Amy said.

"Great thinking; let's go to Victoria's Secret," Jessica said.

The two women coerced Emily into buying a couple of outfits that made her blush even from the display rack. All three women walked out of the store with new lingerie, lotions, and perfume.

"I can't wait to try this on for Lucas tonight. He's going to go crazy," Amy said with confidence.

"Don't expect Alex and me down until late afternoon tomorrow," Jessica said with a wink.

Emily was terrified even to put her lingerie on. What if Mark didn't like it? What if he thought she was trying too hard? The girls demanded she wear the bright red one, to match her toenails, and give them a full report on Mark's reaction the next day.

She couldn't chicken out, so she'd have to muster up the courage somehow. There was no way he was going to turn her down — she knew that much. She just had to quit being such a wimp.

The three women scoured the mall and ended up buying too much. Most of their purchases were for their children and their men, but they threw in a few new clothes and shoes for themselves as well. Emily felt a little guilty about spending so much money, but she hadn't done any major shopping since she'd gotten Trevor set up for school, so she allowed herself to enjoy the day.

By the time they pulled up in front of the house, it was dark, and all three guys were pacing on the front porch, waiting for them.

"What took so long?" Mark asked, concern showing on his face.

"Oh, Mark, quit being so overprotective. You know it takes us girls a long time to find those perfect outfits," Jessica chastised him.

"You three can carry in our bags," Amy added.

"Except for these," Jessica said with a wink at her husband.

The three men spotted the girls carrying the Victoria's Secret bags, and their irritation instantly evaporated. They knew what that store carried.

"Well, it's really late, and the kids are in bed," Lucas suddenly said with a fake yawn.

"Yeah, I'm ready to turn in," Mark added eagerly.

"Let's go," Alex said.

"You three can sit in the parlor with your father and have a drink. We've been shopping all day and need to have a bite to eat and then clean up," Amy said, and the men all wore heavy frowns.

"Fine," Mark grumbled and followed his brothers into the house with his arms loaded down with bags. He was pleased to discover several belonging to Emily. She needed to go out and spoil herself more often.

An hour later, Mark was done waiting and jogged up the stairs to the room he shared with Emily. He went inside and locked the door. The bathroom door was shut, so he shed his clothes and climbed into the bed to wait for her. He'd missed her and wanted her back in his arms. The intensity of the need coursing through him almost tempted him to laugh, it was so ridiculous.

She'd been out for only one afternoon and evening. It wasn't as if they'd been apart for a week. He figured this was all just so new that they were still completely driven by lust. It had to settle down eventually. Nevertheless, he hoped the hunger never went away completely, and he frankly didn't see how it could. That woman really tripped his trigger.

When the door finally opened and she emerged, Mark couldn't breathe for a few moments. She literally took his breath away. When he finally managed to get his brain and his lungs working again, her scent just about sent him into cardiac arrest.

She shyly walked over to him, wearing two tiny scraps of red lace that didn't hide anything from his view. The garters at the top of her thighs were begging him to roll them slowly down her shapely legs, and the heels on her delicate feet showcased the sultry red polish on her toes to perfection. She was a walking dream, and he had to force himself not to take her in one quick plunge.

She'd spent the time to make herself into his fantasy come true; the least he could do was show his appreciation by fully pleasuring her.

"You are so damn sexy," he managed to get past his parched throat.

She smiled shyly at him. "You like the outfit? The girls insisted I get it," she said a bit self-consciously.

"*Like* is not a strong enough word," he gasped. He stood up to walk the few feet over to her, and she could see his obvious approval. He was completely naked, and his full arousal was all the evidence she needed.

Emily gained more confidence and pushed him back down to the bed, so he was sitting on the edge. She stood between his thighs and slowly brought her lips down to his. He reached up to pull her down to him, and she shook her head. "No touching," she whispered in his ear and then licked the lobe.

Mark shuddered as her warm breath caressed the sensitive spot. He obediently placed his hands on the bed beside him, although it almost killed him. He was getting quite a charge out of the game she was playing and was determined to let her carry it out.

She licked the side of his neck and then nipped at his pounding pulse point. She soothed the area with her lips and then made her way up the side of his rugged cheek, until she finally placed her lips back against his. When she brushed her tongue across his bottom lip, he obediently opened his mouth, allowing her access. Her tongue tangled with his as she stroked his arms and chest with her hands. She rubbed her womanhood against his pulsing erection, and he almost jumped off the bed. He started to reach for her again, and she pulled back and shook her head.

Mark moaned out loud as he obeyed her again. "You're dazzling, Emily," he whispered as another wave of pleasure washed through him. She smiled seductively and then slowly pushed him back on the bed. His legs were still hanging over the side, and she bent over him to kiss her way down his throat.

She continued kissing her way across his muscled chest and flicked her tongue over his nipples. He jumped as she nipped the sensitive flesh and then smoothed it out with her tongue. When she lowered her head to continue her path down his stomach, he groaned out loud. He couldn't take much more. Her seduction was going to end without having him inside her.

When her hand enclosed his ridged arousal and rubbed at the sensitive head, he cried out. "Emily, please."

"Please what?" she said breathlessly. She was so turned on by seeing his reaction, she wasn't going to be able to hold off much longer herself.

"I can't take much more before this ends prematurely," he cried.

She smiled at him and then took him into her mouth. The sight of her red lips surrounding his pulsing erection made him tremble. He could feel himself start to lose it. He tried to reach for her again, but she shook her head, making her mouth rotate on him. He wasn't going to make it.

Her hand gripped the base of him tightly, and her mouth took him deep inside. He was a goner. She pulled up and dipped down again, and he cried out as the orgasm rocked through him. She kept stroking his erection, drawing out the pleasure. When she finally pulled back and licked the still-sensitive head, his entire body shook.

"Baby, I'm sorry. That wasn't supposed to happen," he said as she crawled up to him. She just smiled and started stroking him from head to toe.

"Yes it was," she said with a devilish light to her eyes.

"You'll be the death of me," he groaned before playfully flipping her onto her back. "Give me a few minutes to torture you, and you'll be singing a different tune," he said as his tongue started doing magical things to her neck.

He kissed his way down to her barely covered breasts. His hands kneaded the silky mounds, and then he bent his head to suck the peaks through the thin material of her lingerie. She gasped out at the sensation. He finally tore the delicate fabric away and sucked the peak into his mouth. His tongue danced around the pink nipple, which made her back arch off the bed.

As he took turns sucking on each nipple while rubbing the other one, he was shocked to find his satisfied body responding again. He was growing hard in anticipation of plunging inside her. He couldn't seem to get enough.

He moved his lips down her body until he reached her belly button. His tongue swirled in and around it while his hands stroked lower still. He pulled her legs apart and then buried his head between her moistened thighs.

The first stroke of his tongue on her sensitized nub brought her off the bed. He ran his tongue all over her, kissing her soft pink folds intimately. He was ready to take her in a matter of seconds.

He dipped his fingers inside her, feeling her wet heat surround him. She gyrated her hips to take him in deeper. He started pumping his fingers faster in and out as his tongue swirled around the hardened nub. "Mark!" she called out as her body started to convulse around him. He slowed his hands and tongue and then nipped the inside of her thigh.

She collapsed on the bed, limp, breathing heavily. He slowly kissed his way back up her stomach. He stopped at her breasts and gently ran his tongue over the peaks before continuing up to her neck.

He nestled himself inside her thighs and slowly sank himself deep within her. She gasped as she felt his throbbing manhood completely fill her. He could see the surprise in her eyes that he was ready for her again so soon.

He began moving slowly in and out of her, pleasuring them both. They could now take their time and draw out the ecstasy. She started groaning, and he captured her lips once again as he continued the slow, deep strokes inside her heat.

She wrapped her legs around him so he could penetrate even deeper inside her. Their breaths both became short and labored as his rhythm started to increase. The feeling of his chest rubbing against her sensitive nipples was causing her pressure to build.

The feel of him inside her, touching her everywhere, was taking her back over the edge. She raised her hips up to meet him, loving the rhythmic pounding of their hips in the oldest dance of all time.

Her nails raked down his back as he kept kissing her, mimicking the motion of their bodies. He finally gripped her hips to increase the speed of his thrusting. He was pushing so fast and hard, she knew her body would pay the next day, but at that moment, she just wanted more.

"Harder," she gasped as he pushed into her. He groaned out loud and then obeyed her. He thrust into her a few more times, and her body started shaking with her release. She gripped him tightly as the spasms overtook her.

He cried out her name as he shot his release deep inside her, with her body clenching around him. As he tried to get his breathing under control, he clasped her close against him, refusing to relax their connection.

His strength slowly returning, he finally managed to roll over onto his side, taking her with him. He stroked her back for a while, kissing her gently. He took in her swollen lips and looked down to see her reddened hips, where his fingers had gripped her.

"Emily, I'm sorry. That was too rough," he apologized.

She looked up at him with an awestruck expression. "Are you kidding me? That was amazing. You are amazing. I've never in my life had such amazing sex. I know I keep saying *amazing*, but there's just no other word for it," she said with a purr.

She kissed him deeply to make him fully understand. "Thank you, Mark, for showing me how a woman is supposed to be loved," she said, meaning every word and proving she meant it.

Mark visibly relaxed. "If you give me about a week, I can show you again," Mark said.

"I don't think I can possibly wait a week," she told him as she brought her hand down his body and rubbed him.

"Woman, you *are* trying to kill me," he said as he kissed her again. They spent the next several hours kissing, touching, and laughing. No one emerged until very late the next afternoon.

Chapter Twenty-Three

"Mark, I found a lot of pictures of Emily in Chris's belongings. I'm going to do a search on him and see what I can find out. Keep an eye on the guy; I should have everything back within a couple of hours," Chad said.

"I will," Mark replied, deciding Chris would be working with him that day.

Mark walked out to the barn and found Bob with Chris and some of the other guys. "Hey, Bob; I'm going to steal Chris from you. I need help with the south pasture," Mark said.

"No problem, boss."

Chris followed Mark out to the field and they began working the fence line.

"Do you like working here, Chris?" This was something he asked all of his men, but Mark was tense as he waited for Chris's answer. He'd never gotten a bad vibe from the man, which made it worse. Could an Anderson be slipping?

"It's a good job," Chris responded as he huffed while pulling pounding some nails.

"How many other ranches have you worked on?" Mark made sure to keep his voice friendly. He didn't want to give anything away.

"This is the first ranch. I've done a little of everything. I like wandering, not staying in one place too long."

That was a suspicious answer. Mark was becoming more nervous, thinking he'd made a serious mistake in hiring the man.

"Do you have a family somewhere waiting for you?"

Chris's eyes narrowed as he turned to Mark. "Is something wrong? What's with all the questions?"

Mark always liked to know the men who worked for him, and in his experience, cowboys loved to talk about themselves, so his hackles were rising even more.

"I talk with all the men this way, Chris. Is there something you're trying to hide from me?" He wasn't going to beat around the bush. Whether Chad found something out or not, this guy was getting off his ranch today.

"Sorry. I'm a bit touchy on the family thing," he muttered, backing down immediately.

"Why?"

With a sigh as if he knew he had to talk, Chris continued looking down as he began to speak. "I had a wife and kid. They were killed five years ago at a bank. Some punk-assed kid decided he didn't want to work anymore, and thought that robbing a bank would be easy money. My wife was in there depositing my damn check," Chris growled.

Mark felt an ache in his chest at the man's words. If the guy was lying, he was one hell of an actor. There was raw emotion coming off him.

"I'm sorry." Mark didn't know what else to say.

"Yeah, that's all anyone tells me. The kid was caught and will spend the rest of his life in prison, but that doesn't bring my family back to me."

True, Mark thought. Nothing would seal those wounds back up. To have someone you loved snatched away was unforgiveable.

When Chad approached a few minutes later, Mark was relieved. He didn't want to feel sympathy for a man who could be the one stalking his girlfriend. Maybe the pain had been too much for Chris to bear and now this was his form of revenge on the world.

"Hey, boss; can we go inside? I have some stuff to show you. Chris can come along," Chad said nonchalantly.

Mark knew Chad had found the answers he was looking for from the look he gave him. He was just trying to get Chris away from any other people at that point. Luckily, Chris didn't seem to realize anything was up.

Chad was a smart enough man to have gotten the rest of the family away from the house while they got it all settled. The three of them walked into the den, and a couple of police officers were there waiting for them.

"What's going on?" Chris asked with suspicion.

"That's what we want to ask you," Mark said with venom.

On the table were the pictures Chad had found and a printout with Chris's history on it. The man narrowed his eyes to dangerous slits and glared at Chad. Chad smiled at him with an expression that seemed to say, *Bring it on, buddy.*

"What the hell is this? It's OK to go through people's stuff now?" Chris yelled.

"What are you doing with all these pictures of Emily?" Mark asked in a voice of deadly calm. He was, in fact, the reverse of calm, but he wouldn't let that show to this piece of scum. There was even a picture of him and Emily from the first night they'd made love. She was barely covered and wrapped tight in his arms on the upstairs balcony. Mark was beyond the point of seeing red.

"I can have pictures of whoever I like."

"You can't stalk my girlfriend, Chris, terrorize her, and make her fear for her life," Mark yelled before throwing a couple of other pictures of Emily down that were a clear invasion of her privacy.

Chris's face paled upon seeing those pictures. Chad must have found them in some secret hideaway the man thought was safe. He looked nervously over at the police officers.

"Once I found out you were a convicted felon and on parole, I decided to look around a little deeper," Chad said. "I found your stash of photos below a loose floorboard. I think these would be a breach of your parole."

"The crime was bullshit. I went after the kid who killed my wife," he screamed, quickly losing control.

"I don't give a crap why you're a felon. I care about why you were taking photos of Emily," Mark snarled right back.

"You can't prove those are mine," Chris sneered. "They could belong to any of the guys," he yelled with barely controlled fury.

"Actually, we can prove they are yours, as we also found the camera that took them," Chad countered.

"I can't believe you were able to fool me, and I let you near my family," Mark said.

"I guess you're not so smart, you rich piece of crap," Chris sneered.

There was something he wasn't telling them. Chad picked up the signal, but Mark was so furious, he wasn't seeing anything beyond rage.

"Why did you take the pictures, Chris?" Chad asked, trying to calm the situation down.

"It's none of your business, you bloated piece of meat," Chris snarled.

"Officer, I would like to press charges against this man for stalking my girlfriend," Mark said. He was done having a conversation with the piece of scum.

Chad tried to interrupt, but it was all moving forward. He normally listened to his hunches, but he let it go. They'd caught the bad guy; it was over.

The officer walked up to Chris and started reading him his rights. "What the hell are you talking about? I haven't been stalking her; I only took a few pictures," Chris yelled, cutting the officers off.

No one listened to him, and the officers quickly hauled him from the room. Mark felt as if a fifty-pound weight had been lifted off his shoulders. Chris would be going back to prison for parole violation. He was out of their lives.

Mark was disgusted with himself for letting the man into his home. He normally was a great judge of character. He must have been more distracted than he thought. Now that Emily and Trevor lived there and his nieces and nephews came over so much, he was going to have to start having background searches done on all his employees. There was no way he wanted any more men like that one to slip through and be so close to those he loved.

"Thank you, Chad. You found the man much faster than I thought possible. It might have taken me a long time," Mark said to his friend.

"You know there's nothing I wouldn't do for you," Chad told him.

"You owe me nothing, but I do appreciate that you came," Mark said.

"Well, we'll just have to disagree on the owing thing," Chad told him, then slapped Mark on the back.

"You most certainly are a stubborn man," Mark responded.

"Look who's talking. Are you the kettle today or the pot?" he asked with a smile.

"Yeah, yeah," Mark mumbled and then rolled his eyes.

"I know this guy is the worst kind of bottom feeder, but I have to tell you that something feels off, Mark. I don't know — it's just a gut feeling. Keep your eyes out, OK? I really don't like that you weren't able to pull prints or DNA off the letters."

"I think you've been in the service too long now, and don't know when to accept that the fight is over," Mark said with a laugh. Chad didn't laugh.

"Just be careful. Give me that much," Chad insisted.

"OK. I'll be careful. Don't worry, I won't let anything happen to the people I love."

"I know you won't. You're one of the best men I know." The two men rarely said anything this deep, and as Chad became uncomfortable, he turned toward the door. "I have to get back now."

"I know. How much longer will you be gone?" Mark wanted to know.

"I'm not sure." They talked a few more minutes, and then Chad left just as quickly as he had arrived.

"Now that everything is safe, the rest of us are going to get back to our lives, too," Lucas said when the family returned.

"I appreciate all of you dropping everything and being here for us," Mark said.

"Of course, Brother."

The family quickly packed up and was gone before Emily knew it. She was sad to see them all leave. She had grown attached to Amy and Jessica, and to the sounds of their children filling the halls with laughter.

Emily and Mark quickly got back into their old routine. She offered to move back to her room, and hid her reluctance. When he told her that he didn't want her leaving his bedroom, she was relieved. Trevor was thriving, and their life was proceeding on a gloriously even keel. Emily had to believe that nothing could go wrong from here on out.

She couldn't have been more wrong.

Chapter Twenty-Four

It was a great day. Trevor was out riding with Mark, and Emily was feeling accomplished. Not only was dinner ready to go, but she'd also managed to make several dozen cookies, which wouldn't last the day, two dozen muffins, and a casserole for tomorrow. She could get a lot done when Mark wasn't there to distract her.

When the doorbell rang, she didn't even mind that Edward was doing the grocery shopping for her and she was being interrupted. After she took care of that, it was time for a nice long bubble bath and a good paperback book. She'd earned it.

Answering the door with a smile, a man in a uniform was standing before her with a clipboard that Emily didn't think anything about.

"Are you Emily Jackson?" he asked pleasantly.

"Yes, how can I help you?"

"I have a special delivery for you. Can you sign here?"

"Sure," she replied and signed the piece of paper, thinking it was something Mark had ordered.

"Thank you; you've been officially served," the man announced and walked quickly away.

Emily looked down at the papers the man had handed her. Her ex-in-laws had found her and were serving her with new custody papers. They listed her as being in contempt of court, and if she didn't show up in California by the following Monday, less than a week away, she would be arrested, and Trevor would be taken from her.

Emily immediately began to panic. She didn't want to go to that courthouse, where the judge was in the pocket of her dead husband's very wealthy parents. She knew beyond any doubt they would win.

She started doing some calculations and made the decision she would have to go on the run again. She'd saved most of her income and had enough to get settled somewhere else and survive for several months, but it would run out, and if she didn't find a job quickly, she and her son would be homeless.

She'd been there before and she could be there again. It would tear both of them apart being away from Mark and the rest of the Anderson family, along with all the cowboys she'd grown so fond of, but none of it would matter if Trevor weren't with her.

She didn't want to leave Mark. She already loved him so much, and Trevor was thriving. He would be extremely upset to move away, but he'd have no choice anyway if she went to that hearing. He'd have to live with his vile grandparents, and he'd be even more miserable.

The bond between Trevor and Mark was beautiful, and her son was going to hurt no matter what she did. In this moment, she felt like such a failure as a parent. She couldn't believe she'd allowed herself to become so attached when she knew all along the living situation could only be temporary.

Almost in a trance, she moved to the kitchen, and was sitting at the kitchen table, barely able to hold in the tears when Mark and Trevor walked through the door. She refused to let her emotions bleed through, however. She had to be strong for both her son and herself.

The two most important men in her life were laughing and excitedly speaking about how funny the new horses were while learning to walk around. One of the puppies, which were now huge, was trailing at Trevor's feet. The sight of them made her redouble her efforts to keep the tears from falling.

She turned away and composed her face, not wanting to upset her son. She hated that she would have to pull him away from the ranch, his great school, and the entire family. But it was the only way to keep her and her son together.

Mark knew Emily too well to be deceived. He immediately sent Trevor upstairs to clean up and change for dinner. Once the boy was safely out of earshot, Mark sat down and waited for Emily to speak.

"They found me," she simply said.

"Who did?" Mark asked her.

She realized at that point she hadn't told him anything about her custody problems.

"It's kind of a long story."

"Well, there's no time like the present to start," Mark said with a reassuring tone.

Emily took a deep breath and then began.

Mark said not one word as she explained her terrible marriage and the controlling husband she'd been with. His eyes turned to slits as she talked about her ex-in-laws' attempts to take her son from her. When she finished with the part about the judge being in their pocket, he simply nodded as if he understood.

"I didn't have any other choice but to run away from there," Emily told him. "I had to keep Trevor with me. I know they can provide him with everything money can buy, but they would never give him love. They only want him because they lost their only son and are trying to look like loving and concerned grandparents. They barely acknowledged his existence before. They're nothing at all like your family, Mark."

"I'm sorry you've been through all of that, Emily," Mark said as he took her hand in his. "I wish you had shared with me sooner — I could have been there for you. We could have already had this dealt with."

"Mark, I can't beat these people. They know where we are now. I have no choice but to go on the run," she said, choking back the sob that wanted to break through. She was stronger than this, she reprimanded herself.

Mark said nothing for several moments as she sat there in misery. He sat next to her, stroking her back as she got the last of her emotions under control. He then lifted her chin to look directly in her eyes.

"Emily, do you want to leave?" he asked. He needed to know how she felt. He was going to help her no matter what the answer was, but he needed to know she wanted to be there with him.

"Of course I don't want to leave. Trevor is so happy here, and I love you. I just can't lose my son," she said, exasperated.

In the heat of her passion and frustration, she hadn't noticed she'd told him she loved him. It was the first time. Mark let it wash over him and felt his heart growing. Yes, they would be OK.

"Emily, you don't have to leave. I want you and Trevor here. We are going to get married and go into this custody hearing together — as man and wife. They may have the judge in their back pocket, but you, my darling, are underestimating me. First, we'll try to get the Jacksons to settle, but if they want to fight, we'll fight them. If Trevor's grandparents want to fight you, they are going to have to go through me."

Emily stared at him with a mixture of horror and hope. He'd just proposed — or rather demanded — marriage and promised to keep her and her son together. She didn't know what to say to him.

"Mark, I can't ask you to do that," she finally responded.

"Emily, I love Trevor already as if he were my son. My family loves him too, and we protect our own. I also can't imagine waking up each day without you. I want you here, and I won't let these people pull us apart."

"But —"

"Emily, I'd never planned on marrying before. Then I watched as both my brothers got married and had children and I realized it wasn't such a bad thing. We could be really good together if you'd just give it a chance. If things don't work out for some reason, it's not like you would have to be stuck with me forever," he said with a shrug.

That hurt her more than he would ever know — to talk about their relationship coming to an end as if it were nothing — but he was right. If their marriage would keep her with him longer and keep Trevor safe, she had nothing to lose. She loved him, and he said he cared about her. Weren't so many marriages built on far less than that?

"Are you sure about this?" she asked, giving him a last chance to back out.

"More sure than anything," Mark said and threw her one of his sexy smiles. He leaned over and kissed her with a desire that took her breath away and left her wanting so much more.

"I have a lot of phone calls to make to get this started. We will wed on Saturday. Are you OK with having it here at the ranch, or do you want a church wedding?"

"I would love to have it here. It doesn't have to be anything formal," she said reluctantly. She had always dreamed of celebrating her wedding day with all the bells and whistles and borrowed and blue, but this wasn't your typical wedding, and she couldn't expect to plan anything extravagant in only a couple of days.

Her ex had taken her to a courthouse, not wanting to bother with the wedding. He hadn't wanted to bother with her or Trevor, period. Why had she been such a fool as to marry such a cold man? Probably because he'd put on one heck of a good game.

Mark actually laughed out loud at her statement. "I'm sorry to tell you, Emily, but the second I call my father, this wedding is no longer a small thing. He would never let that happen. Be prepared for one serious extravaganza," he said. "We're talking *huge*." He then left her so he could make his calls.

Emily was skeptical and a bit sad. There was no possible way a huge wedding could be planned in only a couple of days. She didn't necessarily want it to be big; she just wanted it to be magical.

She shook her head at her own selfishness. She shouldn't be disappointed she wasn't going to get her dream wedding; she was getting her dream man, for heaven's sake. She smiled as she thought about being Mark's wife. Even if he was talking about it as a temporary thing, she was still going to be his wife. She was determined to make herself so invaluable and so supportive, he would never want to let her go. So sexy, too? That went without saying.

Emily barely made it through dinner before she went up to their bedroom to lie down. The day's trauma had exhausted her, and she just wanted to nap for a while. She was out before her head fully hit the pillow.

Chapter Twenty-Five

The next morning, Emily awoke to find Mark already gone. That was unusual, as he almost always woke her up by kissing her softly all over her body. She was sure he just had a lot to get done that day, and hoped it wasn't because he was having second thoughts.

She didn't know how he was going to be able to fix everything — how could he beat her ex-in-laws? — but she had faith in him. It was strange how much she trusted him. If he told her it was all going to be all right, she just somehow knew that it was.

She took her time taking a shower and getting dressed, and spent it mulling over what lay ahead. She knew she was going to have to make a lot of plans in order to have at least some flowers and a cake at her wedding. She didn't have anyone to invite, so she didn't need invitations or party favors, but she would ask Jessica and Amy to stand with her.

She wouldn't have them go overboard with fancy dresses. She herself was going to most likely wear a simple church dress. There was just no time to find her perfect fairy-tale gown. Mark most likely wouldn't like that anyway. He was a cowboy and she'd never seen him dress in anything other than jeans and his worn Stetson.

She heard voices as she walked down the stairs and then stopped in her tracks as she entered the den. She looked around her in shock. There were people everywhere, and every available space was covered. No one noticed her at first, and she looked around in wonder.

She heard Joseph before she saw him, "No, no, no, that just won't do," she heard him yell at someone in his overpowering voice.

"I'm sorry, Mr. Anderson. I will get rid of these right away and get the next set," she heard some man say and then saw a little guy with a panicked expression rush by her and out the door.

"I can't believe he even thought that would be good enough for my youngest boy and his beautiful bride," Joseph said to someone.

"Emily, there you are, sleepyhead," Jessica said as she came running up. "I wanted to wake you up an hour ago, but Mark threatened death to anyone who dared disturb you," she finished.

"What is going on?" Emily gasped.

"Plans for the wedding, of course," Jessica said, her tone implying that Emily had a screw loose.

"I don't understand. Why are there so many people here?"

"You can't have a perfect wedding in only three days without an army of people getting things done," Jessica answered.

"I just thought we would have a small backyard wedding," Emily managed to get out as she stared at all the chaos around her. Jessica actually laughed.

"Come on, Emily; you've been around this family long enough to understand they never do anything by half measures. There's no way Joseph would allow his last child to have a *small backyard wedding*," she said through more giggles.

Amy joined the conversation. "Don't panic too much, Emily. I thought I would hyperventilate on my wedding day. I was definitely not expecting the huge event they'd planned. I thought it would be us and a judge, but trust me, I'm grateful now I got my dream wedding. I look through the pictures with Jasmine, and she talks about the beautiful princess in the pictures, which just so happens to be me. I actually did feel like a princess. Let us help you make your wedding day the best day of your life."

"Then I guess I'm in your capable hands," Emily said. She would soon regret those words. The girls dragged her through the house, and everywhere, she soon found, was just as chaotic as the den. She tried so many cake samples, she got a stomachache. She was also measured, plucked, and waxed.

The only part of the day that wasn't overwhelming was when she sat down with the wedding dress designer. He asked her to describe her dream wedding dress and he scribbled notes, trying to keep up. He said it would be worked on night and day to make sure it was perfect in every respect. No,

Emily didn't think it could be done, but she couldn't help but hope.

The designer told her he had several gowns finished that would take some alterations to turn into her dream dress and she had nothing to worry about. Emily couldn't imagine it being the same as the vision in her head, but he seemed sure enough for the both of them.

By the time the day was finished, she was practically crawling up the staircase to reach her room. She was sore from all the beauty treatments and beyond exhausted. She climbed into her big bed and passed out instantly.

The next couple of days were much more of the same. She woke up to a houseful of people and ran from morning to night. She barely caught glimpses of Mark and didn't even know if he was sleeping in the same bed. She couldn't wait for the actual wedding to be over with.

"You're not allowed to see Mark at all today," Amy said as she came bursting into Emily's room first thing in the morning. "His brothers have whisked him off to an unknown location for a bachelor party. The kids are all over at my house and will be tended to, and we are off on the company jet to Las Vegas."

"What?" Emily questioned her, trying to wipe the sleep from her eyes.

"It's the day before your wedding, which means it's time for your bachelorette party," Jessica said as the two girls jumped on her bed.

"I really hope you aren't wearing some of your super-sexy lingerie," Amy added with a giggle.

"Me too," Jessica said and then ripped the covers off. Luckily, Emily had been feeling too exhausted to feel amorous and was wearing her favorite old T-shirt and a pair of boxer shorts.

"Hurry up and get ready; we're leaving for the airport in one hour," Amy said, and then the two girls gave her some privacy.

Emily groggily got up and obeyed. She was downstairs in thirty minutes and incredibly grateful for the fresh-brewed coffee sitting on the counter. She poured herself a large mug and burned her tongue with her first sip.

"Are you excited?" Amy asked.

"We're staying at the Mirage," Jessica added.

Emily thought about it for a few moments and found that, yes, she *was* excited. "I've never been there before," she said shyly.

"Oh, I wish it were for more than one day," Amy said. "There's so much to do. I went there a couple of years ago for the first time with Lucas, and had such an amazing time that he let us stay a few extra days. We saw so many shows, and I hate to admit it, but I got hooked on blackjack and ended up playing until the sun started to rise the next morning. I'm excited to have some girls to go shopping with this time. I love Lucas to pieces, but he can't understand the joys of shopping." She was the picture of excitement.

"Well, let's quit talking about it and go," Jessica said.

"Don't we need to pack anything?" Emily asked.

"Not a chance. We'll buy whatever we need there. We don't want to take anything with us, 'cause then that's less room for bringing our purchases back," Amy said.

"Sounds good to me," Emily said. The three women headed out the door to the awaiting limo and drank sparkling cider on the way to the airport.

They boarded the company jet, and Emily looked around in awe. It was more beautiful than any of the hotels she'd been in. The seats were luxuriously big and comfortable, and there was even a flight attendant on board.

"Hello, ladies. My name is Lana — two of you know me — and I'll be helping you on your short trip," the perky blonde said.

"Hi, Lana," the three girls chimed together.

"What would you like to drink?"

The girls put in their orders, and Lana left quickly. When she returned, she told them breakfast would be served once they were at cruising altitude. Emily stared out the window, filled with excitement as the jet picked up speed and lifted into the air.

"This is just amazing," Emily exclaimed.

"That was my reaction the first time, too," Amy said with a smile. "To tell you the truth, it all still amazes me," she added.

Emily smiled at her gratefully. They reached a certain altitude, and the perky flight attendant came back with some fresh fruit and croissants. "The hot breakfast will be out in a few moments," she said and left them again.

The girls ate their breakfast and made plans for the day. The first thing on the agenda was some major shopping and then a little gambling, followed by a couple of shows. Emily couldn't wait until the luxurious jet ride ended.

They landed in no time and were whisked off from the airport in another limo. They drove down the Strip, and Emily's eyes were glued to the window. She was looking everywhere she could, wishing they were going slower so she could see more of the area.

They pulled into the Mirage and were taken to their luxury suite.

"Mark made the reservation for us," Jessica said to Emily. "I told him it was silly to get such an expensive room, considering we weren't going to be spending much time in it, but he insisted on only the best for his bride-to-be."

Emily was so awed by the suite, she had tears in her eyes. The room was twice the size of her old apartment. It had a huge living room area and three bedrooms. Fresh fruit, chocolate, and flowers were arrayed on the table. She wished she had an entire week to spend just in the suite.

"Time to go," Amy said, barely able to contain her excitement.

"I agree; there's a lot of shopping to do and very little time to do it," Jessica added.

Emily reluctantly agreed and followed her two friends out.

Though Emily was reluctant to leave the luxurious suite, she soon found herself glad she'd done so. The Strip was phenomenal, and she wanted to stop and soak it all up. When they reached Caesars Palace and started shopping, she was hooked.

She'd never been a materialistic person and was still reluctant to use the credit card Amy had placed in her hand, but it was hard not to enjoy the dazzling mall they were exploring.

"Mark said that if you didn't come home with several bags, he wasn't going to be happy," Amy said as she pulled Emily toward an exclusive lingerie boutique. "I think this would be a great place to start," she added with a giggle.

They shopped for several hours, then had their purchases taken back to the suite while they enjoyed a buffet lunch. "I think I'm going to gain ten pounds on this trip," Amy said as she sat back, rubbing her very flat stomach.

"I agree," moaned Jessica.

"I'm not going to fit into my own wedding dress," Emily added with a satisfied smile.

"Well, we'd better go walk off all this food, then," Amy said, and they were off to explore more of the city.

They watched a pirate fight in front of Treasure Island and a volcano explode on the Strip. They took a gondola ride at the Venetian and walked so much that Emily's feet were screaming in agony by the end of the night.

The girls finally stopped in the casino and played some blackjack, helping fill the house coffers with their unsuccessful play, then crawled back to their room to catch a few hours of sleep as dawn was breaking.

The car picked them up at noon. They were all much quieter on the trip home and slept the entire jet ride back. Soon, they were picked up at the airport and headed back to the ranch to be prettified and dressed for the evening wedding.

Emily didn't have time for her nerves to get the better part of her. Before she knew it, she was standing behind a set of closed doors, waiting to walk down the aisle.

At that moment, panic started to set in.

Chapter Twenty-Six

Jessica and Amy were fussing with Emily's dress, making sure everything was perfect. She was breathing deeply in and out, struggling to calm herself, as the music began. She couldn't control the rapid beat of her heart.

She reached up to rub the pounding, hoping it wouldn't break free from her chest. She was scared out of her wits. Her son was already out there, looking so handsome in his little tuxedo. She'd been so proud when he'd told her he was standing up with Mark as one of his best men.

"It'll be fine; take some deep breaths. Jessica and I will walk down the aisle, and then you'll follow us out in about two minutes, OK?" Amy said.

Emily felt instant panic at the thought of going down that aisle on her own. She didn't think she'd be able to do it.

"Wait," she blurted out. "We don't have to do it the traditional way; we can all walk together," she begged the girls.

They looked at each other as if she had lost her mind, saw the panic in her eyes, and then shrugged. "Sure," they said in unison.

"Thank you." She started to regain a little of her composure.

"Hey, it's our job as your maids of honor to get you down the aisle. We wouldn't be doing it right if you ran in the other direction," Amy said with a smile.

"It's not that I don't care about Mark, because I do. I love him so much, it hurts. It's just that…well, this is all so sudden, and he only offered to marry me to ensure that Trevor could stay with me. I'm even OK with that. It's just…what if…what if he changes his mind in a week? What if I fall even more deeply in love with him, and then he realizes he made a huge mistake? I don't know how I'd get through that." The panic was rising again.

"Emily, if you could only see the way he looks at you. It's beautiful and magical and everything every woman dreams of. He loves you more than you can ever imagine. These Anderson men have a really difficult time expressing their feelings, but he loves you. I'd bet my firstborn on it," Amy said in assurance.

"I agree. He wouldn't marry you if he didn't love you. Sometimes you don't need to hear the words; sometimes it's as simple as the beating of his heart when it's pressed against yours, the sparkle in his eyes when he can't turn away from you. The words will come, I promise you. Right now, we just need to get down the aisle before he hunts you down and carries you down it over his shoulder. It would make a great spectacle, but we wouldn't want to ruin your gorgeous gown, would we?"

"Thank you. I needed to hear that," Emily said, one tear managing to escape her made up eyes.

"Of course you did. I don't know how I got through my wedding day. Back then, Alex was a complete butt. I'm so glad I did, though, and he has more than made up for his earlier mistakes," Jessica said.

"Ditto. Lucas demanded I marry him. I should have slapped him upside the head. I don't know how many times he has apologized. I forgave him long ago because he's a man worth loving," Amy confessed.

"You two are beautiful and amazing, and they are incredibly lucky men."

"Don't you dare ruin your makeup," Jessica said as she wiped at her own eye.

The three women laughed and threw their arms around each other. Emily could feel her pulse start to slow down. She could do this — even more, she *wanted* to do this.

There was knocking at the door. "Is everything OK in there?" Joseph asked.

"Everything is fine. We are coming out in a moment," Jessica said.

"Good to hear," Joseph said, and then they heard his footsteps begin to fade.

Jessica stepped out of the doorway with her two new sisters on either side of her. There was a gasp from the audience as the three beautiful women made their way to the stage. Not one of them realized the stunning picture they made.

The men standing at the end of the aisle couldn't take their eyes off the glorious women. Individually, they were absolutely breathtaking, and together they made such a sight, the audience was left in awe.

Mark's chest swelled with pride as he realized that in just a few short moments, the beautiful vision walking toward him would be his wife. He wanted to run to her and haul her into his arms. It took everything he had to stand there and wait for her to reach him.

The ceremony went by in a blur, and before Emily knew it, the preacher was pronouncing them man and wife. Mark took her in his arms and pressed his lips gently to hers. It was slow and sweet and took her breath away.

She felt as if she were floating on a cloud as they made their way back down the aisle and then stood for hours greeting guests. She was on autopilot as they cut the cake and sipped champagne. She wouldn't be able to repeat a word that was said during the toasts. She had ears and eyes for nothing but her husband.

When it was finally time for the dancing to begin, Emily melted into Mark's arms and laid her head against his chest. He gently rubbed her back, soothing her nerves, washing the last of her worries away.

He sang along to the country tune being played by the live band, and she glided along the starlit dance floor like a true princess being courted by her Prince Charming. She couldn't believe a wedding could be so magical or that she was Mark's bride.

"Have I told you how beautiful you look?" he asked.

"Only about a hundred times tonight."

"You're always gorgeous, but seeing you walking down the aisle in that dress has taken all rational thought from my head," he said as he spun her in a circle.

"Seeing you in that tuxedo, looking so striking, has made me want to strip it from you piece by piece," she whispered.

Mark's whole body tensed at her softly spoken words. He pulled her tightly against his body, and even through the layers of silk and lace, she could feel how her words had affected him.

"Let's get out of here," he said urgently.

"That sounds perfect to me," she replied, and taking her hand, he started to lead her off the dance floor. They were hoping to escape before someone caught them.

They both heard a commotion over by the caterer's station and turned to find out what was going on. They heard one of the security guards on staff tell someone to leave immediately before there were consequences.

They both walked toward the commotion to find out what was going on. Emily gasped when she discovered who was causing all the turmoil. She spotted them about two seconds before they saw her.

"Do you really think the judge is going to believe this sham of a marriage, you little slut?" a middle-aged woman spat at Emily.

"What are you doing here?" Emily asked the two people, her body shaking as she went into shock at seeing them.

"We came to get our grandson," the woman said. "You stole him from us, and with your husband barely in the grave, it looks like you found yourself a new man to throw his money at you. You always were a gold-digger. We begged our son not to marry you. We even told him the boy wasn't his. We were shocked when the DNA results came in."

"You had my son tested without my knowledge!" Emily sputtered.

Mark was impressed that the only thing she even bothered to comment on was the violation against her son.

"Of course we did. You didn't think we were going to take the word of some tramp that the boy was really our son's, did you?" the woman spit out. "But it's only like you that you'd marry into a bunch of billionaires who wouldn't know the word *aristocracy*."

"What the hell…?" Mark started to rage.

"Of course," Mrs. Jackson said. "The Anderson family, billionaires of the people. How pathetic you are with all your stupid middle-class values. Family, equality, kindness, charity, all those worthless ideas that ruin order in society. Did you know that our son *had* been engaged to a woman with class? Her family and their social and business circle would have accepted us all."

"He said nothing about that," Emily told her former mother-in-law.

"Of course he didn't," Mr. Jackson said. "It was his little rebellion. He decided to marry a *nobody* to show us. And then he regretted you almost immediately. If he hadn't, of course, we would have cut him off. We were waiting for the divorce, but you got pregnant with that little brat. He ruined all our plans."

"If you don't *really* want anything to do with him, then why would you fight for custody?" Emily asked Mrs. Jackson. She paused as if having to think about what she was going to say.

"You took our son from us; now we will take yours from you."

Mark was stunned by the hatred coming from the woman who used to be Emily's mother-in-law. He'd never been tempted to hit a woman in his life, but he had to fight like hell not to slap this one.

"You won't come near my son. You never wanted him, and you won't use him as some pawn in a game I don't want to play," Emily said with the full force of a mother's protectiveness in her voice.

"You stupid little girl, you can't beat us," the woman spat.

"You try to take my son, and you'll see how I beat you," Emily said, raising her fist.

"We're taking Trevor tonight. Where is he?" the woman said and started moving toward the wedding reception.

"Over my dead body," Mark told her, stepping in front of her to block her way.

She sneered at Mark and then stumbled backward, as he was flanked on either side by his brothers. The three of them standing there made an intimidating sight. All through the unpleasant scene, the woman's husband never said a word; he let his wife do all the talking.

"Security, escort this couple off my grounds. If they fight you in any way, call the sheriff. He's a personal friend and will be here in minutes," Mark added as he glared at the woman.

"Fine. We'll go for now, but enjoy your pretend family, because come Monday morning, the boy will be ours," she said before turning around and stomping away. Her husband followed meekly behind, and the security guards followed behind them both, making sure they left.

"Emily, I'm so sorry that happened," Mark said as he pulled her shaking body into his arms.

"No, Mark, I'm the one who's sorry. You shouldn't have to be involved in this," she said with fire sparking in her eyes. She wanted to hit something, but she had a happier thought. "What she said 'against' your family was really a wonderful compliment, you know," she told her husband.

"I do know. *Billionaires of the people.* 'Get your middle-class values here!' Maybe we should put signs up!" He guffawed, but then he grew serious again. "You, however, didn't deserve any of the things she said to you. Don't let her have power over you by affecting you in any way," he said as he clasped her chin in his gentle hands.

Emily looked into his eyes and realized he was right. If she let the rage consume her or broke down, then she was giving a small victory to the woman. She refused to do that.

"Do you still want to leave?" he asked.

"No, you are right; I'm not going to let her ruin my wedding day. If you'll give me a few minutes to freshen up, I would like to dance some more," she said to him with a brave smile.

"Anything you want," he answered.

Emily walked into the house and began attending to her smeared makeup. As she stared at herself in the mirror, she was surprised by the look of determination in her own eyes.

You're stronger than you thought, she mumbled to herself. She placed a smile on her face and then walked out to enjoy the rest of her wedding celebration with her new family.

Chapter Twenty-Seven

"I'm sorry our honeymoon is being postponed," Mark said as they flew down to California in the luxury jet. This time Emily couldn't enjoy the flight, because her nerves were fried and she was making herself sick with worry.

"Oh, Mark, there's no way I could enjoy a honeymoon with this court case hanging over our heads. I can't lose my son. I know you've told me that everything will be OK, but I have been hiding from these people for so long, and it just seems like this is the end."

"I promise you that he won't spend a day in the custody of another soul. I never make a promise that I can't keep. Have faith in me. Once this is all over with and you feel safe again, I will give you that honeymoon you deserve."

"I don't need some fancy honeymoon, Mark, or this big diamond on my finger. I just need to know Trevor's safe and you're in my bed each night."

"Woman, you are a gift from the heavens," he whispered before leaning over and kissing her with pent-up need. Emily made him feel invincible.

They were interrupted by the perky Lana as she brought their lunch out.

"I know this is petty and mean," Emily said, laying down her fork, "but I'm not comforted by the fact you'll travel at times without me and be alone with that woman. She's far too pretty and nice." Emily gave him a slight pout.

Mark threw his head back and laughed. "I have to say I enjoy this jealous side of you," he teased.

Emily glared at her new husband. He wasn't going to enjoy it when she poked him in the eye with her fork.

"I'm sorry for laughing, but Lana is perfectly harmless. She's very happily married to the pilot in front, so you have absolutely nothing to worry about. Do you really think Amy and Jessica would allow their husbands to travel the world with an unmarried woman?"

The two of them probably felt more secure than she did, Emily thought. But she didn't know why she hadn't asked the girls whether Lana was single. The topic had just never come up in their whirlwind trip to Las Vegas.

She and Mark reached their destination more quickly than Emily had expected and were driven to an attorney's office. They had a scheduled meeting with the Jacksons before the hearing come Tuesday. Mark said he thought he could get them to drop the case, but he hadn't clued her in to what he had that was making him so confident.

She was praying Mark was correct and the whole mess could be left behind them. She wanted nothing more than to have a worry-free and normal life. But she was afraid that after the danger went away, Mark wouldn't think their marriage was necessary any longer.

They'd been married only a few days, and it would nearly destroy her if he asked her for an annulment. Still, she was strong and could make it through anything as long as she had her son with her.

They walked into the attorney's office, holding hands and showing a united front. She was shaking on the inside, but to the people they were approaching, she looked confident and at ease. She was thankful no one could see the pounding of her heart.

"Just breathe," Mark whispered in her ear as they neared the conference room.

"I'm trying."

They were led into a huge room with a square table surrounded by chairs. There were two extremely well-dressed men sitting at one end; otherwise, the room was empty.

Mark led her over to the chairs next to the men and sat down. A woman walked in bringing coffee and tea. There were baked goods sitting out as well, but Emily knew she wouldn't be able to get anything down her throat. She was barely able to sip the coffee and did so mainly to occupy her hands.

"Thank you for arriving early, Mr. and Mrs. Anderson. We have the papers all drawn up, and the investigator's report is here. I think this meeting will go in your favor, and you can put all this mess behind you and get on with your lives," the older man remarked.

Emily was more than ready to hear what these reports had to say. Mark had told her only that a private investigator had been hired to look into the Jacksons' past and current lives.

Mark glanced through the papers and then sat back with a huge smile on his face. "You've done your usual amazing job, Dillon; thank you."

Emily looked at him questioningly, but at that moment, her ex-in-laws walked through the door with their attorney. Mrs. Jackson glared at both Emily and Mark, but she didn't say anything as she and her husband moved around the table to sit across from them.

"Hello, I'm Mr. Abrams, and I'm representing Mr. and Mrs. Jackson," the man said as soon as they were seated. "I'm glad you wanted to meet before the hearing, as this could speed things along. My clients went through the legal system to secure custody of their neglected grandson. Ms. Jackson — um, excuse me, Mrs. Anderson now — thought she was above the law and fled. It's pretty cut-and-dried that she's not fit to raise the child. We have agreed to a supervised visitation schedule, which I think is more than generous, considering the circumstances."

Mark smiled at the attorney and then at the Jacksons. So they thought that jumping right in and going for intimidation was their best tactic. But they had never dealt with a man as powerful as he was. He found he was actually enjoying himself.

He glanced over at Emily and saw the fear in her eyes, and his enjoyment evaporated. He might have been used to dealing with crooked people, but she wasn't, and he needed to remember that. He placed his hand on her leg and gave it a reassuring squeeze to let her know it would all be OK.

"Mr. Abrams, I don't want this to turn into a power match, so we're going to get right to the point. We have documentation here showing what the Jacksons have been doing to my client, Mrs. Anderson, over the last year. We also have witness statements from personal friends of the Jacksons showing they've shown no interest in the child, ever. Here's the video from the wedding showing Mrs. Jackson's true intentions for taking custody of the child," one of their attorneys began.

"This is all hearsay, and you know it," Mr. Abrams said, seemingly unconcerned.

"We also hired a private investigator, who has managed to find some interesting information on how Mr. Jackson runs his business," the attorney said and passed copies of all the evidence. Emily watched as both Mr. and Mrs. Jackson turned white while browsing through the papers before them.

The Jacksons' attorney, who had seemed so smug only moments before, now looked confused as he bent his head to speak privately with his clients. Mark sat back and watched them try to regroup. Their own attorneys said nothing else as they waited for the full realization of the situation to set it.

"This has nothing to do with the custody case," Mr. Abrams sputtered, trying to recover from the shock.

"Actually it has everything to do with the case, Mr. Abrams. In our investigation we found out that when Mrs. Anderson's parents passed, they had a large insurance policy that was put into trust for her son. Her parents were very specific in their will, stating they wanted the money to be left to Trevor to be used for his care. It seems that the attorneys who tried to contact Mrs. Anderson were given false information, making them unable to notify her of her son's inheritance. It also seems that there was no interest on your part to take custody of the child until you discovered that whoever had custody of him also controlled this substantial inheritance. Considering that you are both bankrupt and on the verge of losing everything, this will make a very valid point in front of the judge."

"This is hearsay," Mr. Abrams practically shouted.

"Actually, no. The bankruptcy is well documented. And we have witnesses who will swear under oath that Mrs. Jackson repeatedly spoke of not wanting her grandson, but that she'd take him to get her hands on the money. We also have spoken to a Mr. Chris Paisley, whom you hired to spy on Mrs. Anderson. He managed to get a job working for Mr. Anderson on the ranch, correct?"

"We don't know any such man," Mrs. Jackson said, her face blanching even more.

"Were you aware you were placing a felon in such close proximity to your grandson when you hired him?"

"I didn't hire him!"

"That's not what the records show. He has agreed to testify against you as well, saying that he was hired to get any — what were his words?" the attorney looked down. "Oh, yes, any dirt he could on Mrs. Anderson. If he couldn't find any, then there was a bonus in it for him if he could make some up, or put her in circumstances that would make her look bad."

Emily's eyes widened as she listened to Mark's attorney. The man's voice never fluctuated. He was in control, and he knew it. She was horrified to learn all of this about her ex-in-laws. She'd known they were morally deficient — but this was a whole new level of depravity. She hadn't known people were capable of sinking that low.

She hardly had time to wrap her mind around the fact that her parents had left an inheritance to Trevor. All that time they were running, her son could have been so much better provided for. She knew later that anger would set in, but right now she was in shock.

"You have a hearsay case, pure and simple, and you know it. Most of it will be dismissed instantly as irrelevant," Mr. Abrams said as he tried to clutch at any straw he could. He knew he was losing.

"You're very correct that *some* of it doesn't have anything to do with the custody case, but Trevor has nothing to do with this case either. The Jacksons are trying to take custody for the sole purpose of his inheritance, not out of concern for the child. My client's a loving mother and isn't going to relinquish custody. If your clients want to pursue this matter further, then we will bring all of this evidence to court. If they would like to go ahead and sign these papers here, giving up this battle, we'll leave them alone. I believe that is incredibly generous of my clients, considering the personal trauma Mrs. Anderson has been through. It would be well within her rights to sue them," their attorney said with lethal calm.

Emily was starting to have real hope. The lawyers Mark had chosen were top notch.

"We will return in a moment. I need some time to speak privately with my clients," Mr. Abrams said. He rose from his chair and walked from the room with the Jacksons.

Mark turned to smile at her. "We have them on the run. This will all be over in a matter of minutes," he reassured her.

"Are you sure?"

"They've never wanted Trevor. They only wanted money. They're going to have no choice but to admit defeat," he assured her.

"I don't understand…"

"I didn't know until I looked at the papers just a minute ago. I never would have kept this from you. I was suspicious after they showed up at the ranch. They looked too desperate. It had to be more than we knew. You, Mrs. Anderson, are a very wealthy woman," he said with a smile.

Emily didn't know what to think at those words. She'd never been wealthy and neither had her parents. She was amazed they'd thought of life insurance, or whatever it was that they'd managed to leave for Trevor. She was humbled.

"No. My son is. I would never take from him," she said after a pause.

"And you won't need to." She didn't get to respond to that, because the Jacksons were returning. She eyed them warily as they walked back into the room. They seemed older somehow, and there was no glaring this time around. No one as much as made eye contact as they made their way back to the table and sat down.

"My clients have agreed to sign the documents, as long as you sign a paper saying you'll never pursue any of these allegations or issues," Mr. Abrams quietly said.

Their attorneys looked over at them, and Mark nodded his head yes. "Done," the attorneys said. It was all over within a few minutes, and Emily found herself sitting alone with Mark.

"It really is over?" she asked.

"Yes. They can't come after you again. They've relinquished all rights to Trevor," he reassured her.

"Thank you so much, Mark. I don't know how I can possibly repay you," she gasped. She threw her arms around him and held on tight as the tears of relief washed down her face. He stroked her back as she let the joy and sorrow wash through her.

"I would do anything for you and Trevor, Emily. Anything. I thought you would have figured that out by now." The truth shone in his eyes, and she was left speechless. He was so much more than she could ever have hoped for.

She didn't want to discuss the inheritance, or what came next. She was so fearful that now the danger had passed, he would want to end their impromptu marriage. She didn't want that to happen, so if she just ignored it, then maybe he would, too. Perhaps they'd still stay married, and she could have the happily-ever-after she'd dreamed of.

"Now that all of this mess is over, how about we start our honeymoon?" he asked, delighting her.

But she was torn. She wanted to be rushed off to a romantic location where the two of them could lie on the beach for hours, making love all night, and yet the mother in her needed to hold her son and feel reassured that she and Trevor were truly going to be together, with no chance that he'd be taken away.

Mark saw the turmoil in her face and was one step ahead of her. He'd known she would want to be with her son. He knew Emily better than she realized.

"Why don't we start with a nice lunch? You've barely eaten the last couple of days," he said.

Emily realized she was virtually starving. The stress of the upcoming court battle had completely taken her appetite away, and now, with it over, she could clear out an entire buffet. "That sounds great. I could really use some Mexican food."

"Then I know the perfect spot to take you," he told her and called a cab.

He took her to a great little Mexican cantina, and Emily gobbled down almost the entire bowl of chips and salsa. She laughed a little sheepishly and shrugged at him.

They sat right on the beach with the wind blowing over the patio and consumed more than one margarita and much more food than necessary. Emily felt good. She was still anxious to get to her son, though.

"Can we head back tonight?" she asked Mark.

"I want to show you something first," he said.

"OK," she agreed reluctantly.

He paid the bill and then headed out to the street to call another cab. When it pulled up in front of a fancy hotel, Emily had to fight her disappointment. She did love Mark and always loved being with him, but she wanted to reassure herself her son was safe. She needed to hold the boy in her arms.

She followed Mark inside and resigned herself to seeing her son the next day. She understood — Mark was tired and didn't want to make the return flight home.

Mark went through the lobby and around the back of the hotel, then through a double set of doors. They were standing at a huge pool with slides, diving boards, and fountains. There was even a little bar floating in the middle.

"Wow, Mark, that's the wildest pool I've ever seen," she said, trying to be enthusiastic for what he was trying to do for her. But seeing such a kid-friendly area was making the ache in her chest worse. Trevor would have loved this place.

"I thought you might like that," he said with a wink.

"Mom! Mark! You finally got here," Emily heard her son calling.

She whipped her head around, and running down the side of the pool was Trevor, followed by Jasmine. She saw Lucas and Amy, Alex and Jessica, and the other kids milling around, too.

Her eyes filled with grateful tears. Mark had known she would need to be with her son, so he was giving her a honeymoon *and* Trevor. Oh, she would hold on to this man for as long as he would have her, she vowed. She kissed him gently on the lips before bending down to take her son into her arms.

"Mom, I got to fly on a real airplane with Jasmine and everyone. They gave us drinks with tiny umbrellas in them, and we even got to watch a movie. It was so cool, Mom."

"Wow, Trevor. That sounds so fun."

"I'm going to swim some more with Jasmine. We swim to the spot over there, and then the guy gives us soda in a coconut," Trevor said, trembling with excitement.

"How about you give me a big hug first?" she asked as she kneeled down.

"But I'm all wet, Mom," he said. He looked down at his dripping shorts.

"I don't care. I missed you so much."

Trevor rushed forward and wrapped his little arms around her neck. Emily didn't want to ever let him go. But he started to wiggle, and she released him.

"You weren't gone that long, Mom," he said with a crooked smile.

Mark ruffled his hair before grabbing his arm and pulling him close for his own wet hug.

"OK, you guys are mushy," Trevor said with a big smile. "I'm gonna swim now." He grabbed Jasmine's hand in anticipation of getting away from the wacky grown-ups.

Emily laughed at her son's enthusiasm. She loved that he was having such a great time. She loved that he was so happy, and she loved that Mark was the person responsible for it all.

"Have fun then, baby; I'll keep an eye on you from here."

"Aw, Mom, I'm not a baby," he mumbled and looked around to see whether anyone else had heard.

"I'm sorry, honey; of course you aren't."

Trevor was appeased, so he smiled before turning around and jumping back into the pool with Jasmine. The two children made a beeline for the floating bar.

"Have I told you how completely amazing you are?" she asked Mark as she threw her arms around him.

"I don't think I've ever heard you say that," he said with a sexy grin.

"You're the most amazing man in the world. You think of everything, don't you?"

"I'm thinking I should take you up to our room to change right now," he said seductively as he pushed on her lower back to bring her in contact with his hard body.

"Mmm, see, you're always thinking," she said and rubbed her tongue over his bottom lip. Mark groaned before locking his lips onto hers and gripping her backside so she could feel his desire.

"I hate to break this up, guys, but there are kids all over the place, and you are getting a bit X-rated," Lucas remarked while unsuccessfully trying to hide his laughter.

Mark finally broke the kiss but only to glare at his brother. "We'll be back," Mark growled as he took Emily's hand to lead her to the elevators.

"Poor Lucas; you were kind of rude to him," Emily teased.

"He's lucky he didn't get punched in the face," Mark said.

Mark pulled her onto the elevator, where thankfully they were alone. He slipped his hand under her shirt and massaged her aching breasts while his lips devoured hers. When the bell chimed its arrival at their floor, he dragged her down the hallway and had her in the room in seconds.

They didn't return to the pool for several hours. When they did, Lucas and Alex looked knowingly at the newlywed couple, and Jessica and Amy made their own plans to get their husbands alone ASAP.

Chapter Twenty-Eight

"Let's go, Mom," Trevor said as he jumped onto the bed between Mark and Emily.

"What time is it?" she groggily asked her son.

"It's eight already. We have to hurry so I can have breakfast with Mickey Mouse," he said while bouncing on the bed.

"OK, OK," she mumbled. "Go back over with the other kids so Mom can get a shower and get dressed," she pleaded with her son. He sighed at her as if she were killing him, but he did obey.

"How about I join you in the shower and wash your back?" Mark offered with a wicked smile.

"If you do, we're never going to make it downstairs, and Trevor will disown us both," Emily said.

She was seeing a downside to having her son on her honeymoon. They'd switched hotels yesterday and were now staying in Disneyland Park. To be sure, the kids were all excited, and she had to admit she

217

was enjoying it too. But she was less enamored of getting up early when she'd made love with her new husband half the night.

She and Mark made their way downstairs to the lobby, where the rest of their family was already sitting down. Mickey Mouse was talking to Trevor, who was squealing with joy. Jasmine was smiling up at one of the Disney princesses, and the adults were all gulping down coffee as if it were a lifeline.

"You look tired, Bro," Alex said with a smirk as he and Jessica approached. "Were you tossing and turning on someone, I mean something, all night?" he asked and then winked at Emily. Her face instantly turned a dark shade of red.

"You're one to talk, as I see some pretty dark circles under your eyes," Mark said.

"Hey, some of us didn't get so lucky because of all the kids in our room," Lucas grumbled good-naturedly.

"Thanks for watching Trevor," Emily said shyly. She was embarrassed at the thought that the adults at the table knew what she and Mark had been doing the night before.

"Don't worry, my new sister; you'll be returning the favor tonight," Amy said with a wink.

"Hey, this is our honeymoon; we should be kid free," Mark said.

"Sorry, but fair is fair. In addition, I'm the oldest. So I'm not about to be deprived of a kid-free night while out here," Lucas said before punching Mark on the arm.

Mark had to concede defeat.

Within an hour they were all walking through the gates of Disneyland, and the wonder and excitement on the children's faces was priceless. It was well worth the lack of sleep and giving up a private night.

The eyes of the oldest children, Jasmine and Trevor, went from left to right as they walked hand in hand down the street; they eagerly ogled the numerous shops overflowing with souvenirs and edible goodies.

"May I have an ice cream?" Jasmine asked.

"Of course," Lucas said, and he took her and Trevor inside the fifties-style ice-cream shop.

"But, Lucas, it's only ten in the morning," Amy called.

"We're on vacation. There are no rules," he called back, and Amy laughed.

"That's why Jasmine asked him and not me," she said.

"If you noticed, Trevor didn't even look at me. He just went right along with Lucas and Jasmine," Emily said with a smile.

This day could have been so awful. Her son could have been ripped from her arms. But instead, she was in the most magical place on earth with her son, Mark, and most of the Anderson clan. Nothing would upset her.

Wait! she said to herself, chortling. It's technically the second most magical place, after Mark's bed, but that wouldn't have been an appropriate venue for all of the people there.

"OK. We're all set. It's time for me to whup somebody's butt on the Buzz Lightyear ride," Lucas said as he joined them with his own large ice-cream cone.

"I'll take you on, Brother," Mark piped up.

"Isn't that a children's ride?" Jessica asked as she looked at her pamphlet then back at the boys in confusion.

The men threw her a pitying look. "It takes skills to beat the aliens, dear, skills," Alex said as he joined Lucas and Mark in herding the children toward the ride, which doubled as a real-life video game.

The kids liked it so much, they insisted on going back three times before they were ready to move on. Then they moved through the park, riding everything for which they were tall enough to gain admittance.

Jasmine was turned into a princess in the Bibbidi Bobbidi Boutique, and she pranced around the park with a huge grin on her face. When a security guard approached her with an autograph book, her eyes widened with delight.

"Can I have your autograph, Princess?"

"You want me to sign your book?" Jasmine replied.

"Well, yes! I love to have all the princesses' autographs," he replied.

Jasmine took his pen and scribbled down her name, then beamed as he walked away.

"Daddy, he thought I was a real princess," she said in awe as Lucas bent down to lift her in his arms.

"That's because you are," Lucas said.

"All three women's hearts swelled as Jasmine laid her head on Lucas's shoulder, a look of wonder shining in her eyes.

The adults spent the rest of the day wearing out the children by taking them back and forth across the park. Trevor insisted on going on the Indiana Jones ride three times. Jasmine wanted to go into the Haunted Mansion and then buried her head in her daddy's neck the entire time.

By the time they all got back to their rooms, no one had any energy for anything other than sleep. They must have walked at least ten miles around Disneyland, and the adults hadn't been blessed with their own strollers to fall back on, so it was difficult to tell who was more tired, the children or the adults. Poor Amy and Lucas didn't benefit from their kid-free night.

The next day, his brothers were heading home and taking Trevor. Mark needed to get at least a couple of nights alone with his new bride. He had plans for an exotic getaway.

*****

Emily waved goodbye as the family climbed into a waiting limo and headed for the airport. She and Mark were going to catch a commercial flight, since the others were using the jet. When he took her through the terminal, she discovered to her surprise and delight that they were heading down to a resort in Mazatlán. She'd never been to Mexico.

Their suite in the luxury resort had a balcony with a panoramic view that showed both the beautiful Pacific Ocean and the private pool. A concealed hot tub sat in the corner with just enough space for the two of them to sit together and enjoy the stars.

She rubbed her hand over the silk bedding and couldn't wait to crawl in with Mark. He came up behind her, putting his arms around her waist. He started caressing her flat stomach and slowly inched his way up to her instantly aching breasts.

He nipped and licked at her neck, and she leaned back into him to allow easier access. One of his hands made its way back down her body and started stroking her from the outside of her thin shorts. She could feel the warm heat pooling in her core.

She tried to turn around in his arms, but he trapped her where she was. One hand slipped inside the waistband of her shorts and was suddenly rubbing her swollen, sensitive flesh as the other continued playing with her hardened nipple from outside her shirt. He caressed her neck and ear with his mouth.

"Please, Mark," she begged. He groaned but still wouldn't let her turn. He stroked her over and over again until she was falling apart in his arms, then he flicked his finger one last time, sending intense shudders through her entire body. When he gently sat her down on the bed, she was finally able to see his face.

Emily sighed in pleasure, her body relaxed and more than satisfied. The man knew how to turn her world upside down in a matter of minutes. Yet being at face level with his obvious erection started stirring her insides again. Mark wasn't asking for anything, but she could see the effect their playing had had on him.

She knew exactly what she could do to relieve him. Slowly, she began to unbutton his pants; he laid his hand over hers to stop her.

"That was just for you," he said through gritted teeth.

Emily smiled up at him as she pushed his hand away and continued with his buttons. "And this will be just for you," she said before she took his throbbing manhood deep into her mouth. He cried out in pleasure as his hands gripped the back of her head.

She took him deeper inside, loving the feel of his hot and pulsing flesh filling her mouth, and touching the back of her throat. "Emily, I can't…" he began to cry out when she felt him shake hard and felt his release wash down her throat. She licked along the length of him and gently nipped the head before finally letting him slip from her mouth.

He fell across the bed, pulling her with him. "I love you," he said quietly while stroking her hair.

She stilled as she let the three beautiful words flow over her. She looked deeply into his eyes to see if he was going to panic. He just smiled and moved his lips to gently kiss hers.

"Oh, Mark, I love you more than you could ever imagine," she said.

They lay together for a while, enjoying the feeling of being in each other's arms.

"I'm starving," she finally said, as her stomach lodged a formal protest. He laughed and pulled her off the bed.

"Let's take a quick shower, eat, and then go exploring," he said, feeling charged.

"Sounds great." Their shower ended up being less than quick, but she didn't care. When she was in his arms, all her hunger was for him and not for food.

They finally made their way around the city. Enchanted with all the shops, Emily loaded Mark's arms with souvenirs. She had to get something for everyone, after all. He was so patient, he even agreed to the big straw hat she insisted he wear. New bridegrooms, he said, had to take one for the team.

In the cool of the evening air, they strolled barefoot down the beach, letting their feet soak in the warm ocean water. Enjoying the moonlight and listening to the sounds of laughter surrounding them, they never allowed their hands to separate, creating a feeling within her of being treasured and wanted.

She wasn't looking forward to leaving their small piece of paradise.

As the night wore on, they ate a candlelit dinner at a little outdoor diner right on the beach. As the waves crashed rhythmically against the shore, Emily reveled in her newfound happiness.

She looked around at the other couples with their heads bent close together. Some were whispering sweet nothings, while others were locked in passionate embraces. The location was an aphrodisiac, and she was completely pulled in.

As Mark and Emily made their way back to their suite, she felt anticipation burning in her stomach. She couldn't believe how much she always wanted her new husband. When they weren't making love, she was thinking about it. She was ready to fall into his arms at any moment, and she knew that what they had was special.

He ordered champagne and strawberries from room service, and they lay on the bed, drinking and nibbling the berries, with the juices running down their bodies. He slowly began to lick up the mess she was making.

Her breathing deepened as he dipped into the cleavage of her shirt and sipped the sweet juice. He slowly began undressing her, kissing every inch of new skin he exposed. She was primed to take him inside of her in seconds.

His lips began trailing down her exposed flesh, and when goose bumps appeared from the exquisite pleasure, he licked them away.

"Mark," she sighed.

He made his way back up her body, until their lips were once again dancing together. She slipped her tongue inside the moist recesses of his mouth and loved the shudder that ran through him. Her hand strayed down to his erection and rubbed the length of it through the fabric that almost concealed it from view.

He yanked the rest of their clothing away and then covered her body with his. He slipped inside her wet folds and sighed as he buried himself as far as he could go. Emily wrapped her legs around him as he began the gentle, rhythmic thrusts, bringing her close to completion before stopping, drawing out the torture for both of them.

Raking her nails down his back, she pleaded with him to go faster.

"Patience," he whispered and nipped her neck.

When he leaned up on his arms so he could push deeper, she ran her tongue along his hardened chest, making him gasp. He finally gave them what they both wanted and crushed his lips to hers as he sped up his rhythm.

She was convulsing around him, crying out his name as the waves of pleasure washed through her. "Mark," she cried out again as the sensations took her over the edge.

He exploded inside her, pulsing over and over again. He lay there, his weight almost crushing her, but she didn't care. She could lie like that forever.

She once again fell asleep in her husband's arms, feeling at peace with the world.

Chapter Twenty-Nine

"Don't be afraid." Mark was doing his best to coax Emily into going parasailing.

She was terrified and thought her husband had lost his mind. Why did men feel that they had to inflict their ridiculous daredevil exploits on people more sane than they were? She had no desire to be strapped to the flying tarp, as she referred to it. They were on a boat in the beautiful ocean, and he had the brilliant idea that they should go parasailing.

"Trust me; you're going to love it. There's no other experience quite like it," he insisted.

Without Emily's really being aware of what was happening, she found herself being strapped into the contraption she'd been desperately trying to avoid.

"I can't do this, Mark," she said in a panic.

"If you don't do it, you'll have regrets. Close your eyes, and the scary part will be over before you know it," he said and then added insult to energy by smacking her on the butt.

Emily glared at Mark — first the helicopter, and now this! — and then with a determined look gave the OK to the boat captain. He seemed to know he couldn't give her time to change her mind, because the next second, he was speeding up, and she began her ascent into the air.

Her breath whooshed out of her at the sensation of flying. She was terrified at first, but as she reached the full length of the rope and realized it wasn't that far, her fears started to fade, and she found she was enjoying feeling the ocean breeze running through her hair.

It was unlike anything she'd ever experienced. She started laughing at the sheer joy of flying through the air above the Pacific. She wouldn't admit any of that to Mark, however. He was too cocky as it was.

Mark could see the laughter on Emily's face and asked the captain to keep her out there a while longer. He'd known that once she tried it, she'd think it was great. The first step in any new adventure was always the hardest.

When the captain began to bring Emily back in, Mark saw the disappointment cross her features. After she'd made it safely to the boat, Mark asked whether she'd enjoyed herself. She tried to play it cool and then gave up and threw her arms around him, thanking him for talking her into it.

"You can wipe that smug look off your face," she said as she playfully slapped him on the butt, as payback.

"I wasn't saying anything," Mark said in self-defense.

"You didn't have to; your face says it all."

"Sorry about that," he said, still unable to wipe the smile away. Emily gave up on her mock anger because she was having too much fun even to pretend to be upset.

"Do you want to do it again?"

"Can I?" she asked excitedly.

"How about we go together?"

"That sounds perfect," she answered. The crew hooked them both up, and soon Mark was holding onto her hand up in the air, and the experience was even more exhilarating with him beside her.

"Look over there," Mark said.

Emily turned her head and then gasped as she saw a school of dolphins leaping from the water. The incredible animals rose into the air and seemed to hop across the water. They were talking to each other and looked like a group of kids playing.

When the crew brought Emily and Mark back down, Emily was once again disappointed. She found she had a new favorite activity and didn't want it to end.

"Can we do that again tomorrow?" she asked him.

He just laughed.

"Next time you don't want to do an activity, I want you to remember this moment, and maybe you won't fight me so hard," he said with laughter.

She refused to notice the comment but didn't let it affect her.

"I am a woman of adventure," she declared when they went snorkeling. She was beginning to overcome her natural fears.

Emily grabbed Mark's arm as she gazed down into the water and pointed below her. Mark watched as a turtle glided by. He pulled her into another location and pointed out the schools of colorful fish that were in session.

By the time they emerged from the water, they were both waterlogged and wrinkled. They had lunch under an umbrella and rehydrated their pathetic skin.

As they sat at the table, a small band approached and serenading them. Delighted, Emily searched her purse to give them a tip.

"Thank you," she told them.

"No, thank you, pretty senorita."

Another vendor stopped by with a basket of roses, and Mark bought every last one for her. She blushed as the other patrons all clapped at the romantic gesture.

"You're much too beautiful to have only one color rose."

"You're far too romantic to be real," she replied. She leaned across the small table and kissed him softly.

"Ready to head to the room?" he asked, a new light in his eyes.

"I'm very ready, but you've promised me *romance*, and I want to go dancing."

"You're very right. Let's enjoy the pool for a while, and then I'll take you to a salsa club," he said with a wiggle of his eyebrows. They lay out by the pool, soaking up the last few rays of sunshine before the brilliant colors spread out over the skies as the sun set.

Back in their room, he once again tried to talk her into staying in, but she was determined to go dancing. He took her to a smoky club, and as she looked around, she was grateful it was dark, because the way people were dancing made her blush.

"Let's dance," he whispered huskily into her ear. Emily followed him out onto the floor and fell into his arms.

He began a game of seduction, and she was a willing participant. His hands rubbed along her back and up her sides, brushing against her breasts. His mouth trailed down her throat and then back up to her lips, so he could tangle their tongues together.

"Mark, you make me feel so…" she gasped as he pressed his hips into hers. She moved her hands from his neck, gripping his hips, to pull him even closer. He groaned as he mimicked lovemaking with her on the dance floor.

They played with each other, anticipating the night to come, building up their desire, so when they did finally come together, it would be with an explosion.

"We have to leave now, before I forget we're in a public place," Mark growled into her ear and then licked along the lobe.

"I'm ready whenever you are," she purred and playfully wiggled her hips against him a bit more, just to test her power over him. By his reaction, she had quite a bit of control. He had rather less.

Mark led her out of the club and hailed transportation. He had no patience for the long walk back to the comfort of their room.

Chapter Thirty

Emily awoke to the welcome smell of fresh coffee and hot food. She certainly needed refueling after their adventurous day and night. So she climbed from the bed and slipped on her silky robe, feeling extremely feminine despite the loud rumbles emerging from her belly.

"How did you sleep, beautiful?" Mark asked as he came from the other room to join her at the table. She already had her mouth full of food and had to swallow before she was able to answer him.

"I kept getting woken up for some reason," she teased.

"I can't imagine who would do such an inconsiderate thing."

"I would have to say, though, if I keep getting satisfied the way I have been, it's most definitely worth losing sleep over," she said with a seductive twist to her lips.

"Then maybe we should try again."

"I need nourishment," she gasped happily and then bit into a juicy piece of mango. Some of the juice dribbled down her chin, and Mark was right there to clean it up.

"I can't seem to get enough of you," he growled before carrying her off to their bed. They stayed there for a very long time.

Surprisingly, they had enough energy left to spend the rest of their last day on the beach. Mark showed her a few new sites, took her for a romantic lunch, and of course arranged for her to go parasailing again. By the time they headed back to the hotel, Emily was once again ready to collapse into the bed. She couldn't imagine a more perfect honeymoon.

*****

As Emily and Mark prepared their bags to be taken downstairs, Emily felt sadness creeping in. How could she possibly return to the real world? She'd loved her time alone with Mark and was afraid that by stepping back into their normal lives, they'd lose a piece of the magic they'd created.

The ride to the airport was silent as Emily took in everything she could before the inevitable plane ride. Mark could see her disappointment and gently massaged her back as they rode through the streets of Mazatlán.

She glanced out the window and saw a couple flying through the air on a parasail and sighed. She could easily stay there in the city for another week or even a month. Correction. She could if her son were with them. She was already missing him, and that made going home more bearable.

They walked through the airport and were in their seats before she knew it. The flight attendant offered them a drink, and soon, they were up in the air. A tear slipped down her cheek as she watched the Pacific slowly disappear beneath the low-hung clouds.

"I'll bring you back any time you want," Mark tried to soothe her.

"It's not that, Mark; it's just been such a wonderful time being alone with you."

"We will have plenty of time to be alone together," he reassured her.

"You promise me?"

"Baby, I'll be begging you to run off alone with me," he said with a wicked smile. Some of her tension and sadness disappeared as she looked into Mark's eyes. Maybe things would stay the same even with reality intruding on them once again.

"It's just…" She didn't know how to complete her sentence.

"You know that you can tell me anything, right?" He patiently waited for her to speak.

Here goes nothing.

"Well, we married because Trevor's custody was at stake, but now…" How was she supposed to complete that sentence?

Mark leaned back as he looked at her. She couldn't tell what he was feeling by the expression in his eyes. Did he want an easy out? Was he waiting for her to tell him it was OK? She didn't want to end their impromptu marriage. Maybe they hadn't gone about it the proper way, but she loved him, and he'd told her he loved her. Was it enough?

"Do you not want to be married to me, Emily?"

She felt like a goose caught in the sights of a hunter. She knew the bullet was zipping toward her, but she couldn't figure out how to get out of its path. Wouldn't it be better to just tell the truth? Before she was able to say anything, Mark sighed and began speaking again.

"We found out that you have a substantial inheritance. You can easily take care of yourself and Trevor. I won't like it, but I will respect your decision, whatever you decide." It seemed as if the words had been torn from his chest.

He didn't seem as if he wanted her to leave. Hope was rising within her as she looked at the pained expression on his face. Fear had kept her from admitting how badly she wanted to stay with him, but she was more fearful of not being with him.

"I like where I am," she mumbled. That hadn't given too much away.

Mark raised an eyebrow and waited for more. When she didn't say anything, he gave her a crooked smile. "Well, then, we shouldn't rock the boat."

What the heck? "We shouldn't rock the boat?" she finally muttered.

"Yeah, things are good. I'm happy being with you, and you're happy being with me, so we should just leave well enough alone." He seemed quite satisfied with his conclusion.

How freaking romantic, she thought. But then again, it wasn't as if she were giving him much, either.

"Fine. We won't *rock the boat*," she said with the slightest trace of sarcasm.

"Good. I'm glad we got that over with," he muttered just as the flight attendant walked up.

They ordered their drinks, and then Emily leaned her head against Mark's shoulder, grateful when he wrapped his arm around her and tugged her in close to his chest. Yes, they would just leave well enough alone. There was no need to discuss something that neither of them wanted to discuss. She was happy just being married to him and having a secure home.

Her tension eased and Emily slept the rest of the flight home.

Chapter Thirty-One

Trevor was out in the yard, playing with the puppies. Mark chased them with the hose, and Trevor ran away and squealed happily, with two huge puppies at his heels.

As Mark doused them with water, the puppies started to yap, and Trevor fell to the ground giggling; the puppies pounced and immediately licked him all over his face. Emily couldn't help but laugh along with them.

She'd been reluctant to give up her fantasy world in Mexico, but they'd been back for almost a month now, and things had grown better each day. Mark hadn't pulled away from her as she'd feared he might. He found excuses throughout the day to come into the house and steal kisses and chat with her as she worked in the kitchen.

She had a secret to share with Mark but wanted to wait until she knew for sure how he'd react. She thought he'd be happy about it, but there was a small piece of her mind that was insecure. She rubbed her still-flat stomach, already protective of the child growing there.

She loved her son so much and knew she would love her new child with an equal passion. Especially when she had no doubt that Mark would make an amazing father, and would never be disappointed with his child — never too busy to spend time with him or her.

Her two favorite men burst through the kitchen door, soaking wet and laughing so hard, there were tears rolling down their faces. It was so good to see the utter joy on Trevor's face. Her ex had tried to squelch any amount of laughter in their home, yelling at Trevor for interrupting or just making him go away. The man had always been focused only on playing with his rich friends. Like him, none of them had or wanted jobs; all of them just wanted to have fun, and a wife and kid didn't fit the definition.

She really should have left him long before he died. Had she known that men like Mark existed, she surely would have. Both she and Trevor deserved so much more than her ex had ever given them. They deserved a man like Mark.

"You're getting my floor all dirty," she scolded them, doing her best to sound strict. She tried to keep the stern expression on her face, but their pitiful looks worked their magic on her. "Go get cleaned up, and come back with the mop," she said with a smile.

They rushed out before they could get into any more trouble.

She couldn't let them think they could mess the house up, or she'd be living in a mud pit. Still, as she listened to their laughter fade away as they stomped up the stairs, she thought that she'd rather live in a mud pit than a home with no joy.

Emily laughed as she continued to work on their dinner. She'd been having some horrible morning sickness and had missed making breakfast for the hands a couple of days that week. Though no one was complaining, she wasn't happy with herself. It was her job to cook, and that she was married to the boss didn't mean she didn't take it just as seriously as before.

She was making it up to the guys by making extra-special dinners and sending them off with leftovers to snack on later. They told her that if she kept cooking such good dinners, she could miss breakfast every day.

Mark stopped her paychecks and put her on all his accounts. She'd tried to insist on keeping things separate, but he wouldn't hear of it. He told her everything he had was now hers, too. She didn't feel comfortable with that. She also didn't feel right getting into her son's inheritance, so she'd let Mark put it into a great mutual fund. By the time Trevor went to college, he would have no troubles at all.

Mark told her he was looking for another cook because he wanted more time with his wife. She'd stubbornly refused to accept anyone else. Several people had come by for interviews, and she'd managed to find something wrong with each one of them. It didn't help that they'd all been women and a few of them much too attractive to be around her husband daily.

She wasn't the jealous type, but why bring someone into their home who was so tempting, especially since she was going to be getting huge very soon?

She knew it would be nice to have someone share the cooking, especially since she wasn't feeling well, but she loved to do it and was afraid that if she allowed someone else in, she'd be completely pushed out.

She made a decision that if the perfect person came by, it was meant to be; if not, her husband would have to deal with missing her.

The hands all decided to barbecue at the bunkhouse that night, so she finished making them salads and sent everything down with Trevor and Mark. They'd told her she didn't need to make them anything, but she would have felt guilty if she hadn't.

As Mark, Trevor, and Emily shared an intimate dinner alone — something rare when you lived on a ranch — Emily relaxed and ate with her first real appetite in several weeks.

"Mom, you and Mark are married now, right?" Trevor asked.

"Yes, baby, we are," she said. He must've been really distracted, because he let her get away with the pet name.

"Does that mean we're going to stay here forever?" he asked again while looking at his plate. She was unsure where he was going with the conversation.

"Yes, Trevor, that's what it means," Mark broke in.

Trevor smiled at Mark with the happiest expression she'd ever seen pass his little face.

"Does that mean you're my dad now?" Trevor asked shyly. Emily held her breath, not knowing what to say.

"I'm your dad if you want me to be," Mark said with a little crack in his voice.

"Then can I call you Dad?" Trevor asked.

The next words Mark spoke could make or break her son. Emily held her breath without realizing it.

"Nothing in the world would make me happier or more proud," Mark said and held his arms out to Trevor. Their son jumped out of his chair and rushed into Mark's arms. Mark squeezed him tightly to his chest.

"I love you, Dad," Trevor said, and a little tear slipped from his eye.

"I love you too, Son," Mark said while holding on tightly. Emily couldn't stay seated, so she stood and wrapped her arms around them both, joining in the hug. They really were a family now. She could no longer keep her secret to herself.

"How would you feel about having a baby brother or sister?" she asked Trevor.

"I think that would be OK," her son said after giving it a little thought.

"I think it would be more than OK," Mark said. "Do you want to get working on it?" he added with a waggle of his eyebrows.

"We don't need to work on it," she said and laid her hand against her stomach. Mark's eyes widened as he realized what she was telling him.

"You are?" he said in awe. She nodded her head *yes*. He jumped up from his chair and lifted her off her feet. He spun her around as he laughed with joy.

Her head started spinning a bit, and she pleaded with him to put her down.

"I'm so sorry; are you OK?" he asked as he rubbed her back.

"I'm fine, Mark; maybe a little less spinning though," she said with a smile. He smiled back at her sheepishly.

"I can't wait to tell my family," he said excitedly. "Not only do I get one son, but I soon another child as well. Thank you so much for all you've brought into my life."

"You're the one who should be thanked. You've given us so much — most important of all, you've made us a real family."

"Let's compromise and agree we're all great together," he said.

They finished their dinner together, and then sat by the fire watching a comedy. The evening ended on a perfect note, with laughter and snuggling on the couch.

Life was good.

Chapter Thirty-Two

"Good morning, young lady. I hear congratulations are in order." Joseph, who had walked into Emily's kitchen unexpectedly the next morning, was smiling from ear to ear.

"Thank you, Joseph. Yes, you'll have a new grandchild in about eight months." A radiant smile lit Emily's face.

He corrected her. "I have a new grandson now, since Mark submitted papers to officially adopt that beautiful boy of yours. Then I'll also get the added bonus of another grandchild in eight months."

The acceptance of her child into the Anderson clan filled Emily with pure joy. If anything were to happen to her, he'd still be a part of their family, and they'd always take care of him. That was the greatest gift any mother could receive.

"Thank you for being who you are, Joseph. You will never know how grateful I am that you hired me to work here. I don't think there are words to express my gratitude." Emily had to stop, as her throat was starting to get choked with emotion.

"Oh, Emily, I'm the one who is grateful. You have brought a light to this place that it hasn't seen since my grandmother left this world. You're truly a joy and your young Trevor is a ray of sunshine. I am so thankful my boy was smart enough not to let you get away," Joseph said in a suspiciously tight voice before stepping forward and wrapping Emily in a warm embrace.

Emily clung tightly to the huge man, laying her head on his chest while he patted her back. The moment made her miss her father so much, she couldn't stop the flood of tears from escaping. She blamed it on the pregnancy hormones.

Physically, Joseph and her dad — who'd been a small man — were like night and day, but the two of them were equally blessed with the virtues of kindness and generosity. She missed him and her mother, too. But how lucky she was to find Joseph and Katherine and get a set of grandparents who would love her son, and a mother- and father-in-law who would love her.

"I'm sorry, Joseph. I wasn't trying to weep all over you," she said as she pulled away and went to the sink to wipe her face and get control over her emotions.

"Ah, lassie, it's OK. Sometimes a good cry can fix anything," he told her with a kind smile.

"I am discovering that," she said with a smile.

"Well, I was stopping by today to let Mark know that I'd found him the perfect cook and maintenance man, and that's when he gave me the great news," Joseph said.

Emily's eyes narrowed. "Who is this person?" she asked. After all, Joseph had been the one to find *her*, and she really didn't want a young woman to be there all day.

"It's actually a married couple. They've worked for the company for many years but want something different now. I told them about Mark's needing another cook, and they asked if he could use a maintenance man as well. With a place this big, two more people would be a blessing, especially with Mark's growing family," Joseph said.

Emily knew it sounded a bit selfish, but she did not want to share the house with two more people. She loved having Edward there, but he always gave them privacy, and most of the time, you didn't even know he was around. It would be much harder to get any privacy with her husband if two more people moved in.

"Mark has a little cottage right around the corner. They could live there, and you wouldn't have to share your newlywed space," Joseph said with a wink.

Emily turned scarlet as she looked up at him. She was a little worried the man was a mind reader, among other things.

"I didn't know that was there."

"It was built years ago for a married couple who worked here, but it has been empty for some time. We'll have to bring a crew in to fix it up, but they could start in about a week if you like them," he said.

"It wouldn't be up to me."

"Of course it's up to you, Emily. You're the lady of the manor now. Mark already knows them; they're coming over for you to interview."

"Oh" was her response; she didn't know what else to say. It made her a bit nervous to be the one responsible for the employment of two people. It also made her heart thump to know that she was the lady of the house. She'd never really thought about that before.

The couple arrived about an hour later, and Emily fell instantly in love with both of them. They were in their early fifties and full of life. Mary had as much passion for cooking as Emily did, and she knew they'd work well together. She also knew that if she wasn't feeling good, Mary would be perfectly capable on her own.

Scott was Mary's husband, and although he was quiet, his face lit up when Trevor came into the room. He explained the two of them hadn't been successful in having children, and so they both took great joy in spoiling everyone else's kids.

When Mary prepared a meal with Emily, it was as if they'd always worked side by side in a kitchen. It was just one of those perfect fits, and Emily was more than happy to offer Mary the job.

"I would love it if you worked here," Emily said to her after visiting for a while longer. She couldn't offer Scott a job, as that was Mark's area, but she knew they were a package deal, and according to Joseph, Mark had already approved of them both.

"I think we're going to work wonderfully together," Mary said, then gave Emily a hug.

Mark came in and invited Scott to come over to the cottage with him. The two men were going to figure out exactly what the place needed and get the right people out there immediately. Emily was eager for the week to pass and the sweet couple to move in.

When she'd woken up that morning, she'd hardly thought she would feel that way, but life had a way of working out for the best.

Chapter Thirty-Three

And Emily was right. She'd been fighting morning sickness for a week straight, and shortly after the new couple had moved in, Mary had whipped her up a magic drink that completely cured her. Mark had made a couple of serious mistakes in hiring, but he was now on his game.

Emily was sitting at the table with her feet up and the magic drink in her hands. Mary had insisted that her boss rest until she was at a hundred percent, and had made the whole lunch on her own. The men were enjoying Mary's cooking as much as Emily's.

The incredible aroma of lunch cooking led the men to tramp into the kitchen, where they sat down at the table, bringing in nonstop laughter, talking, and mud.

Emily loved every minute of the busy ranch life. She felt completely at home, and each ranch hand had a special place in her heart, especially since David, the creepy one, had disappeared when she and her husband were gone on their honeymoon.

Mark walked through the door with his usual tagalong, her son, right behind him.

"Mom, we're going to rope calves today," Trevor said excitedly.

"That sounds fun."

"Yeah, and then we're gonna cas... cas... What are we gonna do again, Dad?" Trevor asked as he looked at Mark. The men around the table snickered as Mark looked uncomfortably toward Emily. She could see he didn't want to tell her. She just raised a brow and waited.

"We're going to castrate them," Mark said. Once the word was said, the laughter stopped and all the men groaned. It seemed a word no man wanted to say or hear.

"Oh," Emily said and felt herself blushing.

"It's just all part of ranch life," Mark said with a shrug, trying to get on with a new topic quickly.

"Isn't he too young to do that?" Emily asked with concern, not letting him off that easy.

"He's a big guy," Mark said and patted Trevor on the head. Emily didn't have the heart to say no to anything her boys wanted, so she let it alone.

"This stew sure is great," one of the guys said in between huge bites.

"Well, you have Mary to thank," Emily said. "She did all the cooking today. As a matter of fact, I think the special ingredient is Rocky Mountain Oysters," she said with a laugh.

The men looked up in horror before seeing the grin on Emily's face, then they smiled big before turning to Mary.

"Thank you, Mary," they all chorused together.

"You're very welcome. Tonight Emily and I are preparing her famous enchiladas."

"Yessssss!" the men shouted. Emily didn't see how they could have that look of hunger in their eyes while they were finishing a hearty lunch, but she supposed they burned a massive amount of calories in their jobs. She was just grateful to be needed and appreciated.

The guys inhaled the rest of their food and then headed out the doors as quickly as they'd come in.

"I'm getting quite attached to those boys," Mary said as they all left.

"I know how you feel," Emily said. The two women cleaned up the dishes and started prep work for dinner, easily falling into conversation, the time fading fast.

Mark sneaked back into the kitchen a couple hours later, stole a kiss, and then vanished again. She loved that any time he found himself near the house, he came in, even if it was for less than thirty seconds. She loved how much he loved her. Nearly as much as she loved him.

The routine of their days offered comfort and happiness. Mark stayed closer to the house and let his ranch hands get more of the tasks done as he worked with Trevor every available moment. Emily spent her time in the kitchen, but she would sneak out with her boys any chance she got.

Over the next couple of months, her stomach started to round slightly, not enough to show much but just enough to prove a baby was growing there. Mark would lie next to her for hours in the evenings, rubbing her stomach and talking to their new child.

He was an incredible father to both his children. Trevor adored him, and the baby already had a nursery, thanks to Mark's efforts. Emily was content to spend her days cooking and visiting with Mary and her nights in her husband's arms. She was finally allowing herself to accept the fact that her life was perfect, and nothing was going to ruin it.

*****

"Do you really have to go?" Emily sniffed as Mark packed his overnight bag. He'd been called to Montana for some urgent business. She normally would have gone with him, but Trevor had a field trip the next day and she'd already agreed to chaperone.

"Believe me, I don't want to leave," he said. He stopped packing to pull her close to him and kiss her softly. First things first — and Emily always came first.

Mark slowly undressed his beautiful wife and loved her gently, not wanting to leave for even one night. They hadn't spent a night apart since their wedding day, and every hour without her would be hell.

After they got dressed, she walked with him downstairs. He kissed her one more time before heading out the door. He turned back to see a tear falling down her cheek and almost said to hell with it and walked back in.

"I'll be fine; I'm just going to miss you," she assured him when he paused as if undecided what to do.

"Are you absolutely sure you'll be OK?" he asked while he stood by the car, not yet touching the door handle.

"I already told you, Mark, I'm going to be fine. This is just pregnancy hormones acting up," she assured him.

"I'll be back before you even realize I was gone."

"That's not possible, but I am surrounded by good people and I can go a night without you, even if it feels like I can't. Go do your business and have fun with your friend. I love you, Mark Anderson."

"I love you too, Emily Anderson. I'll call you as soon as the jet lands," he said as he blew her a kiss, then finally got in the car and started it. She maintained her composure so he wouldn't feel any worse than he already did.

She stood watching until the car was out of sight, proud when no more tears fell. But she was engulfed with loneliness. The ranch hands were all out on the north pasture, several miles away. Edward was at his son's house for a few days, and Mary and Scott were doing some shopping. She wasn't normally all alone in the huge house, and she didn't like the feeling.

She decided to go down to the far barn, where new kittens had been born a couple of weeks back. She knew the sight of them would cheer her up until Trevor returned from school.

Emily walked down the now familiar path to the barn and went inside. She lay down next to the kittens and gently petted them, feeling sorry for herself.

"This is ridiculous. You've spent many, many days alone. If you can't suck it up for a few hours, then you are too dependent," she lectured herself in a whisper.

Feeling a little better, she rubbed the head of the little black-and-white kitten and listened to the mama cat purr.

When she was almost ready to get up, she heard a noise behind her, but before she was able to turn around and see what it was, she felt a shooting pain in her head, and all went black.

Chapter Thirty-Four

Mark had reached the airport when his cell phone rang. He picked it up, thinking it would be Emily calling for one last goodbye.

"Hey, Mark; you can cancel the trip. We got the issue solved," said the voice of his friend.

"Are you sure?" Mark asked, but he was already turning his car around to head home.

"Yeah, we got it all fixed. You can stay there, where I know you really want to be," the man said with a chuckle in his voice.

"You got that right. I'd much rather be with my family," Mark said with a relieved sigh.

"What's going on over there in Anderson Land? You're all falling head over heels?"

"We've just discovered it's much nicer to have a beautiful woman at our side every night than to be out trying to find a new girl every weekend," Mark said sincerely.

"I think I'll go ahead and hold on to my bachelorhood," his friend said and then hung up the phone.

Mark pulled up in front of the house, ran inside and called out to Emily. He didn't get an answer, so he headed up the stairs. He smiled as he pictured her lying there in their bed. Pregnancy was wearing her out, so she did tend to take a few naps now and then.

He quietly opened the door and stepped inside. Emily wasn't there. Not to worry. He searched through the house and then the pool and still couldn't find her. He knew she had to be around, because her car was sitting in the garage.

The property was too quiet. He glanced around, then thought of the barn. She was most likely down there playing with the kittens again. He jogged down there and was relieved to see the open doors.

None of his guys would leave the door open, so she had to be in there. He walked through and was stunned when he didn't find her. He crept over by the kittens, and his heart stalled in his chest.

He dropped down to his knees and felt the scarf he knew belonged to his wife. When he examined the drops of blood lying there in the hay, his panic escalated. What had happened? He ran back to the house and called the hospital. Maybe she'd injured herself and called an ambulance to pick her up.

A few minutes later, Mark had no answers at all. It was time to call in help and send out a search party. His wife never strayed far without telling someone where she was. He picked up the radio and had all his men come in immediately. He then called his father, who was to summon his brothers.

Mark organized the ranch hands, and they all took different sections of the ranch. He'd been gone for less than an hour, so she couldn't have gone too far. He quickly thanked God he hadn't gotten on that jet. If he hadn't come home when he did, she could have been out there all day before someone noticed her missing.

Mark shook his head as he realized he was most likely overreacting. She was probably down by the lake, or reading a book not far from the house. Was his fear irrational? He couldn't get the blood spatters from his mind.

After the men had searched every inch of the property, they met back at the house. Mary and Scott had returned and made coffee, tea, and sandwiches for everyone.

"You all need to eat and keep up your energy to find Emily," Mary told them. They all obeyed, even though no one had an appetite.

Every person on the ranch had fallen in love with Emily, and with her missing, the stress was immense. Mark's family arrived while they were making a new game plan, and he was relieved to have his father and brothers by his side.

"I've called search and rescue. They're bringing out the dogs. We'll take them to the barn, which is the last place we suspect her being, and they'll begin tracking her," Lucas said.

"I don't understand where she could have possibly gone," Mark said with his head in his hands. "It's been hours, and she never leaves without letting someone know. Trevor will be home in a few minutes, and she's always here when he walks in the front doors."

"We'll find her, Brother. I promise you," Alex said. He laid his hand on Mark's arm in comfort.

The three brothers continued to talk about different options as the women made call after call, trying to see if she'd been seen anywhere.

A news crew arrived, and Joseph gave them a brief statement and then asked them to put Emily's picture up. When someone who was associated with the Andersons disappeared, it was front-page news. Joseph hated to take the time away from his sons to give a statement, even if it was a short one, but he knew the media could be their friend. Anyone who spotted her would call in. And this was the only way he could get her picture flashed up on every person's living room television.

Joseph finished and then asked them to give his family some privacy. He knew he wasn't going to get the reporters and photographers to leave completely, but he could keep them away from the house.

"Did they leave, Dad?" Mark asked when Joseph walked back in.

"Well, you know they won't leave completely until she's found, but they're at the end of the drive and away from the house," Joseph reassured his son.

"We're going to find her, right, Dad?" Mark asked his father. At that moment, he felt more like a child needing his father's comfort than a grown man with children of his own.

"I guarantee you we will find her and she'll be OK," Joseph promised his son. He prayed to God he could keep that promise.

Chapter Thirty-Five

Emily awoke to a pounding in her head. She tried to lift her hands to soothe the pain and found she was unable to move them. She tried to sit up and couldn't move her body at all. She began to panic and started trying to yank her arms and legs free.

Opening her eyes to view her surroundings, she found she was lying in a dingy bed in a tiny room and her arms and legs were tied down. Terror filled her, and she started to cry.

"Mark," she cried out with a pain-filled voice. There was no answer. "Mark!" she yelled again louder. What was happening?

She heard a noise and at first sighed with relief, thinking Mark had found her. The door opened — a strange man walked through it. She didn't know him, but he scared her to her very core. Beady eyes gazed her way, and her skin crawled at the grime covering his face along with a shaggy, unshaven, narrow face and a pointed nose.

"You finally woke up. I was beginning to worry," he said as he continued gazing at her with wild eyes from across the room.

"Where am I, and why am I tied up?" she asked. Her lip trembled.

"You're home," he said simply.

How was she to respond? Emily didn't want to provoke his anger, but she didn't want him to think she wanted to stay.

"Ummm…I don't understand."

"It's really simple to understand," the man said as he moved closer to her. A shiver of disgust moved down her spine as the man leaned over her.

"We had a special connection, and then you chose that stupid rich man instead of me. You accepted my flowers, you read my love letters, and you still married him. Well, you're mine now, and you won't be leaving here," the man said.

Emily looked at him in horror. This was the person who'd been stalking her? She didn't understand how that was possible. They'd found the pictures of her in Chris's stuff — Chris had been a convicted felon. She stared at this man in confusion as the reality fought to sink in to her befuddled brain.

"I really don't understand, because I've never met you before," she said, making sure to keep her voice calm, and trying to recall the self-defense course she'd taken her senior year of high school. She knew she didn't want to provoke her captor.

"We did meet. You helped me pick out some fruit at the supermarket when you were new in town, and I told you I'd repay the favor," he said.

For the life of her, she couldn't remember the event.

"Peaches. And roses. Roses mean love. You told me you loved me; you see?"

There was a flicker of memory at a man in the grocery store and discussing fruit, but he was nothing like this man. He hadn't been so filthy – so frightening looking. This couldn't be the same man, could it?

"You said it would be nice if I repaid the favor, and you would see me next time. I kept coming back to the store at the same time — I lost my job because I had to be there at the store — but you never showed up, so I sent you the flowers. I watched your face as you accepted them, and you were smiling. I then sent you the notes and letters. I knew you wanted to be with me, but Mark wasn't letting you leave. Then you went and married him and cheated on me, so I've been waiting until I could get you alone," he said.

He was now sitting on the edge of the bed, and Emily was beyond terrified. She was at his complete mercy, with no means of escape. Mark would never be able to find her; *she* didn't even know where she was. She was so scared she was going to lose her baby because of this demented man. She wanted to place her hand protectively over her womb but couldn't move her arms.

"I'm really bad with names; can you tell me yours again?" she asked him, hoping to stall him until she could figure something out.

"It's Joshua, remember?"

"Oh, yes, now I remember," she lied to him.

"See, we did have a connection. I knew if I got you away from that place, you'd remember me," he said as he ran his dirty hand down the side of her face.

"I'm really uncomfortable, Joshua. Can you untie me?" she asked him in what she hoped was a friendly voice.

"Not yet," he said and started to pace. "You could be trying to fool me. My daddy taught me women lie all the time to get what they want," he spat at her.

"Joshua, I wouldn't lie to you," she said.

"Just shut up," he yelled at her and lifted his hand in the air, as if he was about to strike her. Emily shrank away from him, but he never threw the punch.

She lay there silently and cried. She prayed somehow Mark would find her.

"I'm going to make us some dinner, like a real family, and then I will take you outside to use the bathroom, because tonight, you'll finally be mine," he said before walking from the small, filthy shack.

Emily immediately began twisting against her restraints. If she could get one hand free, she could undo the rest and perhaps get away. But the struggle was doing nothing but wearing her out, and she finally decided to save her strength. Her only chance would probably be when he released her to go outside. She'd been a pretty fast runner in high school, so if she could just get loose from him, she might have a shot at getting away.

The biggest problem was that it was already getting dark out, and she had no idea in what direction to run. She didn't care, however. She would run until she just couldn't go any farther and then find somewhere to hide. The darkness would at least conceal her from him. She would wait it out until dawn if she had to. She couldn't stay there and let the man violate her.

She lay there in misery until finally her pain and exhaustion overtook her, and she drifted off into a restless sleep.

"Emily, wake up."

Emily jerked awake to find Joshua lying over her. Her stomach heaved at the smell of his revolting breath in her face, and she gagged, making his eyes narrow dangerously.

"Do I repulse you?" he snarled as his fingers locked down on her jaw and he forced her to look at him. It was taking everything in her to not break down.

"N…no," she stuttered, her throat tight as she looked into his anger-filled eyes.

"Mark has brainwashed you, made you think he's the right man for you, but he's not. I am. You'll see that. You will come to appreciate me. I was so angry when I watched you kiss him, but I knew you were just putting on a show for me. I could tell when your eyes looked out into the woods that you were looking for me. Our eyes even met once when I was sitting in the trees. You had a dreamy expression on your face. I knew you were wishing we could be together. It will be OK. I promise you. That man will never find us."

Joshua bent down and ran his lips across hers, the smell of dirty chewing tobacco and neglected teeth entering her nose and making her gag again.

"You think you're so high and mighty now!" he snapped as he leaned back and lifted his hand, slapping her hard across the face. The sting made her vision blur as she fought against blacking out. Who knew what would happen if she did? Not that she was going to be able to protect herself if he decided to rape her.

She felt hopeless.

"No, I don't, Joshua. I just…I'm not feeling well. I haven't eaten all day," she whispered, fighting to keep the tears at bay.

His demeanor changed as he looked down at her, while lifting his hand again and stroking her sore cheekbone.

"I'm sorry, Emily. I lose my temper sometimes. I don't mean to. You probably are hungry. I'll go finish our dinner. I caught some fat squirrels today. They're cooking up real nice. I went all out for our first night. I wanted it to be special."

"Thank you, Joshua," she said. "Can I use the bathroom first?"

"No. Not yet. It's OK. If you have to go, just go. It don't bother me none," he said as his eyes traveled down her shaking body. "Things are going to get messy later, anyway," he added with a leering grin.

Oh, please, Mark, find me, she inwardly cried as Joshua walked back outside. She wasn't going to give up, but there seemed to be no hope. Her arms were bruised and swollen from tugging so much on the ropes.

She didn't care. She continued to struggle against her restraints. She'd rather die than be taken by that man.

Chapter Thirty-Six

The search team arrived at the house, and Mark led the men to the barn. The dogs smelled the area and then immediately started pulling at their chains to follow Emily's scent. Mark immediately went along with them.

Lucas and Alex were right there at his side, and the three of them followed the search team through the woods. Mark couldn't figure out why she would have come this way unless it was against her will.

About a mile through the woods that bordered his property, the search crew leader stopped, pulling everyone in for a talk.

"I see a cabin over the rise there, and the dogs seem to be leading us straight to it. Now, we don't know if Emily got hurt and sought out refuge or if she was kidnapped, but with the blood and the direct path leading to this place, it looks more like a kidnapping to me," the search leader said.

"Let's go then," Mark said with a growl. If some beast had his wife, he was going to get her back and then rip the man to shreds. Why in the hell were they standing around talking about it instead of marching forward? Emily needed him.

"Mark, I know you want to rush in, but that's not the smart thing to do. We need to sneak up on the property. If someone has taken your wife and he's inside with her and knows we're there, it will turn into a hostage situation. The best outcome for Emily is if we can catch this guy on the outside. We're going to come at the cabin from different directions. Let's do a radio check to make sure your earpieces are working. No one speaks louder than a whisper," the leader commanded.

It was obvious to all involved that the guy was a former military man. Mark was grateful that this hard-core professional was the one in charge of the operation. If Mark did something foolish that put his wife in even worse danger, he would never be able to forgive himself.

They split up and slowly made their way toward the cabin. Mark was with his brothers, and the search leader was coming in from the other side. As they crept closer, Mark heard a commotion, and the dogs went crazy.

"I've got him," Mark heard someone yell.

"Check the cabin," another voice piped in. Mark didn't need any more prompting than that. He sprinted the last hundred yards, calling out Emily's name, and threw open the door, not worried about his own safety.

When Mark looked in the dimly lit cabin and saw Emily lying there, tied to the bed, every instinct in him said to run back out the doors and kill the man who had done this to her. But he couldn't leave his beloved wife for that long. His better thoughts drew him directly to her.

"Mark, I knew you'd find me," she sobbed, as he sat on the bed and gently touched her. He felt all over her body to make sure nothing was broken and then bent down to brush her swollen mouth with his lips. When he saw the bruise forming on her cheek, he felt himself begin to shake with the need to pummel the worthless scum outside.

"I'm so sorry this happened to you, baby," he said through clenched teeth. He began untying her and had to hold the rage in as he saw her reddened wrists and ankles. He couldn't believe what that monster had put her through.

"I'm OK, Mark; you got here before he could hurt me," she said with tears streaming down her dirty cheeks.

"Baby, he did hurt you. I promised to not let anything happen to you, and then I left you alone. I can never forgive myself for that."

"Mark, you are the one who found me. You saved me before he could do any real damage. You're my hero," she told him as she lifted her hand and touched his cheek.

There was a tear falling from his eye. He hadn't realized he'd allowed his emotions to get so out of control. Holding the rest back, he lifted her up onto his lap and held her close. He continued to rub her back and run his hand over the small bump on her belly.

"The baby?" he asked, afraid of her answer.

"The baby is fine; I've been feeling movement, but I definitely want to go get a checkup right away. He hit me pretty hard on the head."

Mark could see the dried blood on her beautiful hair, and his whole body tensed again for a fight. Lifting her carefully, he carried her out of the cabin. He couldn't stand to have her in there for one minute longer.

Soon, they heard the sound of sirens, as the police and paramedics were coming down the overgrown dirt driveway. Mark held her in his arms until the ambulance came nearer. He quickly walked over to it and laid her gently down on the stretcher. The paramedic hooked her up to some machines, and soon, the sound of their baby's heartbeat could be heard over the chaos all around them.

Mark breathed his first sigh of relief since discovering she was gone. He glared over at the kidnapper, who was currently being secured by two police officers. Knowing Emily was safe, Mark found himself walking up to Joshua, who looked at him with loathing. Uncaring of the consequences, Mark's arm lifted and he punched the man hard in the jaw.

Joshua slumped as his eyes rolled back in his head. Lucas quickly grabbed Mark before he went in for the kill.

"Let's stay focused, Brother," he murmured.

The two officers standing there acted as if they hadn't seen a thing. Mark didn't even care. It would be worth a night in jail to beat the bloody hell out of that man.

"Let the law deal with him," Alex said as he helped Lucas pull Mark away. "You need to be there with Emily."

Hearing Emily's name snapped him from the all-consuming rage, and Mark's shoulders slumped. Yes, he needed to be there for his wife. As much as he wanted to bloody the man who'd hurt her, that wouldn't help her now.

"Mr. Anderson, we have some questions we need to ask both you and your wife," an officer said as he approached Mark.

"My wife needs to go to the hospital right away; can you please follow us there?" Mark said, and he moved back over to Emily. She hadn't seen what he done, thank goodness.

"We can do that. This guy is getting taken into lockup, so he won't be harming anyone else tonight, or ever again once the law is finished with him," the officer said and then walked away.

"If you have it under control, we're going to jog back over to the ranch and meet you at the hospital," Lucas said as he looked calmly at Mark.

"I'm good. Thank you," Mark said. Lucas patted him, then his two brothers began moving through the woods back toward his ranch.

Mark felt better as the ambulance started making its way to the hospital. He would feel much better when they confirmed that everything was OK with both his wife and his unborn child.

Emily was rushed into ER and, soon after, she was seen by a doctor who happened to be a friend of Mark's.

"She's going to be fine," Dr. Harison told them. "I want you to keep an eye on her tonight while she's sleeping because of that bump on her head. It looks like you got really lucky in finding her so quickly," he finished.

"Thank you, Jim; I appreciate that you saw her so fast," Mark said as he shook the man's hand.

"You know I would do anything for you, Mark," the doctor said and then left.

The doctor had given her some pain pills, so her head wasn't pounding anymore, but she was sore, and her wrists and hands burned. She wanted nothing more than to shower the grime off her body and then sink into a bubble bath. If she hadn't been pregnant, she'd have wanted the water boiling, she felt so filthy.

Mark helped her dress, and she had to smile at the irony. He was usually trying to get her out of her clothes, not put them on.

"This is a change," she said with a small smile.

Mark looked at her in shock as he realized she was joking with him. "I love you, Emily. I can't even think what could have happened if we hadn't found you when we did," he said with a thick voice.

"Mark, you did find me in time, and I simply don't want to think about that man or place anymore. I'm one of the lucky ones who *was* found, and it's because I have you," she said as she ran her hand over his cheek.

"OK, just for you, I'll try to stop worrying," he said with a weak smile.

"Thank you. Now let's go home." He took her hand and led her out to the ER waiting area. Lucas and Alex jumped up as soon as they spotted them.

"Are you OK? Is the baby OK?" they asked in unison. Emily nodded her head yes and then on impulse hugged each of the brothers. They each wrapped an arm around her and cradled her to them protectively.

"Thank you for caring about me. I'm glad to have brothers like you," she said as a tear slipped out. Both men were too choked up to say a word and instead hugged her just a little bit tighter. A few minutes later, they made their way outside to the car.

The men were treating her like a porcelain doll. Mark even placed his hand on her head as she bent down to get in the car, worried she might bump it.

She sat snuggled up in Mark's arms in the backseat on the ride to the house. When they pulled up, the front door opened, and the porch filled with her "sisters" — Amy and Jessica — and Joseph and Katherine, Mary and Scott, and Edward.

She was once again overcome with emotion as she looked at the amazing group of people who were her family. She walked up the steps and was engulfed in hugs and kisses and then led into the den, where she sat down with a blanket arranged over her and a steaming mug of one of Mary's magical elixirs placed in her hands.

"You drink this up, and then we'll get you upstairs to clean up before you have to do any talking," Mary said, taking over like a mother hen.

Emily obediently drank the soothing liquid and realized it did make her feel better and seemed to give her the added energy she really needed.

When she finished the drink, Amy and Jessica led her upstairs, and she was ecstatic to stand under the soothing spray of hot water. She took a long time washing away all traces of her captor and her captivity, and she turned her skin pink from the violent scrubbing.

By the time she stepped out and put on some clean flannel pajamas, she was feeling almost human again. "Please burn those," she said of the mud-covered clothing she'd been wearing.

"No problem," Jessica said. She whisked the clothes off the floor and threw them in the wastebasket, saying, "They will be gone before you come in here again."

The women made their way back down the stairs, and Emily was once again settled on the couch with a warm blanket placed over her. Mark sat next to her and pulled her tightly against his side.

Emily told them how she'd been in the barn and the man had approached her from behind, hitting her in the head — she didn't know with what.

"Where did he come from?" Jessica asked. "I thought we'd caught the bad guy."

"So did I. Apparently you have to be careful who you are nice to in the grocery store. My first week or two here, apparently I helped him in the produce aisle. I remember almost nothing about that, but whatever I said must have had an impact, because he told me we had a connection. I've seriously never been that scared," she said with a shudder.

"You don't have to talk about it anymore, baby," Mark assured her.

"I'm OK now, Mark. I'm home with you and our family. I can get through anything as long as you are all here," she said. That she meant the words so fully surprised her.

"That's what family is for, to lean on in times of distress. We're always going to be here for each other," he assured her.

"I know that now. I know it more than anything," she said as she held her chin up so his soft lips could caress hers.

"You are so unbelievably beautiful."

"I don't look very beautiful right now," she said with a sigh.

"You look more beautiful than ever," he corrected her, then kissed her again.

"OK, I'm starting to get a little bit nauseated here," Lucas said with a laugh.

"Oh, you hush; that is amazing," Amy scolded him.

"I'll show you what amazing is," Lucas said as he lifted her in his arms and kissed her breathless.

When Emily looked up, she realized Trevor wasn't there, and a new panic set in. She needed to see her son.

"Is Trevor OK?"

"We didn't tell him what was happening. We thought that would be best. He's sleeping right now, and we've been checking on him regularly," Joseph said.

"Thank you, Joseph; I wouldn't have wanted him to know," she said. Though she knew the boy was safe, she planned to check on him when she went up to bed.

"I know you're all worried and waiting for me to fall apart at any moment. I was terrified beyond anything when I was locked in that cabin, but the terror ended the minute Mark walked through the door. I knew somehow he would be there to save me, and I want you to know you really don't have to worry about me," she told them, feeling comforted as Mark's arm tightened around her shoulders.

"OK, we'll quit the worrying," Jessica said. "Well, we might worry a little, but we'll be sure to hide it from you," she added with a laugh.

"Everyone can either use guest rooms here or head home, but I'm taking my wife up for a nice long bubble bath to ease her aching joints, and then bed," Mark said to his family.

"I think we'll head home and hug on our children for a while," Amy said as she walked over and embraced Emily.

"That sounds like a great idea," Emily told her.

"We'll do the same, but we're coming over this weekend with the kids so we can have a big family barbecue," Jessica told her.

"Perfect. Thank you, Jessica," Emily said, excited to have the family over for another get-together. That's what she needed. She wanted to put this behind her, push it to the furthest reaches of her memory, and move forward. That would be most healing.

"Your mother and I are going to stay the night. We'll feel better in the morning if we get to spend time with our grandson," Joseph said. He and

Katherine gave Emily a kiss before heading off to the stairs.

"I love you guys," she called after them.

"We love you, too, Emily, so very much," Katherine said as she took Joseph's hand and climbed the stairs. Katherine didn't speak a whole lot, but when she did, the love and reassurance in her voice made her words special.

"I'm going to make you some dinner to eat after your bath. I'll leave it on the table by the door. It will be something easy on your stomach," Mary said and then rushed off to the kitchen.

"I really am grateful that you're OK. Since you've come into this old home, there's noticeably more laughter. You're a beautiful woman inside and out," Edward told her.

"Thank you, Edward. All of you are my family. I'm so sorry you had to cut your visit with your kids short," she said and then kissed his cheek. He mumbled something and then walked away.

"You, my beautiful wife, are incredibly loved," Mark told her when they were finally alone.

"That's the greatest gift I could have ever received," Emily said to her husband.

Mark lifted her into his arms and gently carried her to their room. Having put her on the bed, he drew her a warm bubble bath. He slowly stripped the clothes from her body and kissed her sweetly before carrying her into the bathroom, softly releasing her into the soothing water.

"Do you want to join me? I could use a foot rub," Emily asked him. Mark stripped his clothes off and climbed into the opposite side of the tub. He lifted her foot into his lap and began to gently massage it.

Mark rubbed her feet and slowly massaged his way up her shapely calves and thighs. All thoughts of the day were washed away as Mark stroked her, from the soles of her feet to the top of her thighs and back down.

He turned her around and gently washed her back, then brought his hands around and ran his soapy fingers along her stomach and over the mounds of her breasts. She leaned her head back into his neck and let the sensations of his touch wash over her. She could feel his arousal pressing into her back and had to smile at how masculine her husband was.

He finally rinsed them both off and carried her, still wet, to the bed. He ran the towel over her, making her ache for him. He then tucked her into the bed and pulled her into his arms.

"You know how much I love you, right?" he asked her, as he gently kissed her lips and throat.

"I think as much as I love you," she answered him and then groaned.

"I think I was in love with you from the first second I saw you and Trevor standing there, so beautiful, after I'd been through such a rotten couple of days," he told her as he continued to slide his hands across her body.

"I fell in love with you the first time you talked kindly to my son," she said with tears in her eyes.

"Oh, Emily, how could I not love him? How could I not love you?" he said.

He showed her how much, long into the night.

Epilogue

Joseph sat in his chair, watching all his grandchildren tear open their Christmas gifts. He was cuddling baby Tassia close to his chest. She was only a few weeks old and as beautiful as the rest of his grandkids. Mark and Emily certainly had the right recipe for a beautiful baby.

Watching Trevor and Jasmine sharing chocolate raised a smile. Jasmine had been disappointed to find out that she couldn't marry Trevor, because he was now her cousin, but she soon recovered when she found out their new relationship meant they got to spend more time together.

Isaiah and Katie were each rocking on their brand-new wooden horses, and their giggles made the whole room light up.

Katherine was playing Christmas songs on the piano, and all the children were singing along. When

Jessica's beautiful voice was accompanied by Amy and Emily, it sounded like angels from above.

Joseph's three sons were sharing a drink by the fire, and every few minutes they would glance over at their wives as if to make sure the women didn't disappear on them.

Joseph was filled with pride at the wild success of his matchmaking. He now had the large family he'd longed for, and if things kept going as well as they had been, he'd be blessed with even more grandchildren.

One source of disappointment, however: he didn't have anyone else to match up. And he was such a master of the game.

"Dad, come have some of this cognac; it's really good," Lucas called to him.

"Give me a minute," he said. He reluctantly got up and placed Tassia in her portable bassinet, standing over her, making sure she didn't wake. But if she did, no problem — he'd be more than happy to pick her up again.

She stayed asleep, giving him no excuse to cuddle her close again. He walked over to his boys and held his hand out for a glass.

"I have to admit, Dad, Christmas keeps getting better and better each year," Mark said. Once again, he looked over at his wife and son.

"I thought marriage would be the end of my life, and yet I find it was only the beginning," Lucas admitted.

"I never thought I would take the plunge, but without Jessica, I'm only half a person," Alex said.

"Of course, all those wonderful babies sure make the holidays bright again," Joseph added as he glanced around the room filled with music and laughter.

"I hate to admit you were right, Dad, but we're going to have to give you one," Lucas said.

"Well, that's sure nice to hear every once in a while," Joseph said while puffing out his chest a bit.

"Merry Christmas, everyone," Alex said to all his family. The room was filled with choruses of Merry Christmases, and Joseph knew life was as wonderful as it could possibly ever be.

"Mr. Anderson, you have an urgent phone call," his butler said as he stepped into the room.

Everyone went silent as Joseph picked up the phone.

After a few moments, Joseph's face blanched. "George, slow down. Tell me what is wrong." A few more minutes of silence. "I'll be right there, Brother."

Joseph hung up the phone and turned toward his waiting family. "That was your Uncle George. He wouldn't tell me what it was, just said that he needed me," Joseph said as he moved toward the stairs.

"Well, then, we're going with you," Lucas said; the sounds of others agreeing could also be heard.

"Of course you are. Family always comes when we need each other."

The room cleared out; their uncle needed a share of their comfort and joy.

The Anderson Family Continues in

The Billionaire's Marriage Proposal

Excerpt:

Prologue

"I see you've been busy the last several years, Joseph."

"Aw, very much so. I love my growing family," Joseph replied with a twinkle in his bright blue eyes.

"We both know it was your meddling that led to all those grandkids of yours," George said with a little jealousy.

George Anderson had finally come home after five years of grieving the loss of his wife. Since he and Joseph were twins, they had an incredibly strong bond, but losing the love of his life had been too much for George. He'd needed to retreat from the world for a while. Joseph was relieved to have him back.

"If you hadn't been hell bent on going off to see the world, then maybe you'd have a bunch of your own grandkids," Joseph said.

"I came to you for help. Those kids of mine are never going to settle down and you've obviously had success with your own," George said.

Joseph had grown tired of waiting for his sons to find brides, and give him grandkids, so he'd taken matters into his own hands and found good mates for the boys. They were still clueless to his sneaky ways. All three of his sons got married within a few years' time, and now Joseph was a happy grandfather. He felt sorry for his brother, knowing George was feeling the same sense of emptiness he'd felt only a few years ago.

"Nothing would give me more pleasure than to help you," Joseph said with enthusiasm.

"I know with your help, I'll be holding my own grandkids in no time. Life has been hard for me since I lost my beautiful Amelia," George said.

When George lost his wife of forty years, he'd been unable to stay in the home he'd shared with her for most of his life. They'd married at sixteen years of age and he didn't know how to live without her.

"Are you doing any better?" Joseph asked. He couldn't imagine losing his Katherine. She was the light of his world. Without his wife and kids, life wouldn't be worth living.

"I take it a day at a time. If I had grandkids to distract me, it would make it easier. Since their mother's passing, the kids have become distant, with each other and with me. I'm afraid if something doesn't change soon, we'll completely break apart," George said in a voice laced with pain.

Joseph got them a drink, giving his brother time to compose himself. He poured them each a shot of bourbon before coming back to the chairs by the fire where they were sitting.

"Why don't you stay with me, here? You can look for a place and relocate to Seattle. I think what you need is a fresh start. I know we can get your kids to follow. We'll fix this, George. Trust me," Joseph offered.

George looked at his twin brother, considering his offer. He'd lived in Chicago his entire adult life and it was a bit overwhelming to think of moving permanently, but change may be exactly what he needed. Chicago was filled with too many depressing memories of the loss of his wife.

"You know what, Joseph? I think I'll go ahead and do that. You still have a guest house, right?" He asked.

"You're more than welcome to stay there for as long as you like, or you could stay in the main house. There's too much space in this big old place."

"This is your home with Katherine. I'd much rather stay in the guest house until I find a place - it shouldn't take me long. Now, what plans do you have for those kids of mine?" He asked.

"Tell me everything about my niece and nephews. The more I know about them, the more likely I'm going to find matches that they won't be able to resist," Joseph said. The two brothers sat by the fire until the early hours of the morning, and made plans.

By the time they finished talking, Joseph knew what he was going to do with his eldest nephew, Trenton.

"Ah, it really does feel good to be matchmaking again. I was kind of sad for it to end with Mark," Joseph said with a smug look on his face. "But, don't you dare let on to Katherine or I'll be sharing the guest house with you."

The two brothers had a good laugh before heading to bed. Joseph was eagerly anticipating the months to come. He wouldn't mind the pitter patter of great nephews and nieces alongside his grandkids.

Chapter One

"Your father is on line one, Mr. Anderson," his assistant called over the intercom. Trenton sighed. He hadn't spoken to his father in months and couldn't understand what he'd need.

"Thank you, I have it," he replied. He took a moment to clear his thoughts before picking up the phone. He knew he'd need his wits in full before taking the call.

"Hello, Father. What can I do for you?" he asked coldly.

"Is that any way to talk to your father?" he asked. Trenton could hear the hurt through the phone line and he cringed. His mother had been the glue holding their family together and since she'd passed he'd hardly spoken to his father or siblings. He didn't know if he even remembered how to anymore. They used to be close but had all withdrawn when their mother passed. They had to protect their hearts from the unbearable pain, somehow. She'd be so disappointed in them.

"Dad, we've barely spoken in the last five years. Why change anything, now?" Trenton asked.

"I can see this is going to be harder than I imagined. I'll just get to the point, then. I've moved the corporate headquarters to Seattle. The paperwork went through today. If you still want to run the company you'll have to relocate. You have thirty days to make your decision - before your offices will no longer be available to you in Chicago," George said.

Trenton sat at his desk in shock. He'd never been made speechless before, but his father's news actually left him without words. The line was silent for several moments, while neither of them said anything.

"Why would you do that?" Trenton finally asked with rage in his voice. How dare his father try to control him. He'd run the corporation on his own for the past five years, when his father retired abruptly. The fact his father still had enough control to be able to move the offices had never been a factor, as he'd been a silent owner.

Trenton tripled profits during his reign as president and the corporation was worth billions of dollars. Many lives depended on them to make a living. He didn't see what his father had to gain by moving the corporate offices. Most of their business was done internationally and their home office wasn't significant, but Trenton had grown up in Chicago and had no desire to leave.

"It was time for a change. I've let our family drift apart, but I'm done with that. I'm still the head of this family and this is what I've decided. I know you well, son, and I know the second we get off the phone you'll be calling your attorneys to see if you can put a stop to this. I'll try to save you some time - the answer will be *no*. I may be silent in the corporation but I still have certain rights and if you read through the paperwork, one of those rights is to have the corporate offices wherever I choose, so long as I give the current President a month's notice. So, here's your notice. If you check with your assistant, a fax has been sent, laying out the move and the new building. I'll see you next month," George said. He disconnected the call and left Trenton sitting with the phone pressed to his ear, seething mad.

"Andrea, get in here, now!" He shouted into his intercom. His assistant came running into the room, looking a bit frazzled. She had the paperwork from his father in her hand, knowing he'd want it. She laid it on his desk and stood back for him to read. "You can leave," he dismissed her. She quickly exited.

He knew he could be a hard-nosed boss at times, but he felt he was fair. If his employees did their job well, they had nothing to fear. He just didn't tolerate errors or slacking, so if they messed up, there were no second chances.

Trenton spent the rest of his afternoon confirming what his father said. It looked like the old man was right. There was no way he could stop the move. He had enough of his own money that he could tell his father to go to hell, and just start over - but he didn't run the corporation for the paycheck, he did it because it had been in his family for longer than he'd been alive and he had a lot of pride in it.

He hung his head in a rare moment of weakness. He knew he couldn't quit. He knew he'd be playing right into his father's hands, but he'd move with the corporate offices. He also knew that meant a lot of new staff, and a hell of a lot of headaches.

He went home, drank a double scotch, then pulled out his phone. He had to call his siblings, which he hadn't done in over a year. Each of them worked in different areas of the corporation and they were going to be just as furious at their father as he was.

His father may be getting him to move across the country but he wasn't going to get the happy family reunion he was hoping for. Trenton was enraged and he was going to let his father know it.

"Are you sure we've done the right thing?" George asked Joseph.

"I'm sure. The first step in this process is getting the kids together, again. We can't very well match them up if they aren't here, can we?" Joseph asked.

"Trenton's been distant in the last several years, but I've never heard him speak to me so coldly, before. I know losing their mother was hard for all of us, but I should've never let us grow this far apart. I can't believe this is the same boy who used to worship the ground I walked on," George said with sadness.

"I guarantee you, Brother, by this time next year, you and your boy will be together again, and things will be back to normal. I can't say I've experienced what you're going through, but nothing brings a family together more than other family members in their face. They used to be close to their cousins and we'll all have that bond again. Just you wait and trust me," Joseph reassured him.

"I've always trusted you," George said.

"Well that's because I'm much older and wiser," Joseph said, while puffing out his chest.

"You're exactly three minutes older, so don't give me that, again," George said with a laugh.

"Hey, those three minutes gave me a world of knowledge."

"Yeah, I think it gave you a world of arrogance - just like your eldest nephew," George said. He had a feeling everything would be okay. His family was at the beginning of truly mending.

"He did what?" Max yelled into the phone, causing Trenton to hold the piece away from his ear.

"He said it was time for a change so he's moved the home offices to Seattle. We now have twenty-seven days before the official opening in Washington," Trenton repeated.

"You have got to be kidding me. Can we stop this? He's obviously gone insane," Max said, but there wasn't much oomph in his voice. They both knew there was nothing wrong with their father's mental capabilities.

"I already checked every which way to Sunday and there's nothing we can do. I was sorely tempted to tell call his bluff, and leave the corporation," Trenton threatened. Max knew there was no way that would happen - just like he knew the same of his other siblings.

Though the siblings had been distant the last five years, they each had a love of the corporation in common, even if they were involved in a variety of different areas.

"Looks like we're moving to the beautiful North West, then," Max said. He was angry, but not nearly as much as his brother. He traveled so much for work that he wasn't home enough to be very upset. Besides, he hadn't spent time with his cousins in years and he missed them.

He'd never admit it to his father, though. The old man was getting his way, and he didn't need to know Max wasn't upset about it.

"Yeah, I can hardly wait," Trenton said sarcastically.

"Have you called Bree and Austin yet?" Max asked.

"No, I called you first and figured we could each take one of the others," he answered.

"Sounds like a plan - I'll call Austin," Max quickly said with laughter in his voice.

"Gee, thanks," Trenton replied. He knew the call to his sister, Brianna, was going to be long-winded. His sister was stubborn and independent and didn't like to be told what to do. He smiled, though, when he thought about what she was going to say to their father. George was in for an earful as soon as Bree got off the phone with Trenton.

Trenton sat back, feeling better after talking to his brother. He and Max had been close in the past and he realized he missed speaking with him. Trenton may not have noticed it, but his father's plan was already working. It had brought the siblings closer, even if it was in uniting them against him.

*****

Jennifer yelled at her computer screen and then looked around with guilt. She hated computers and wished they'd never been invented. They were the worst possible creation and she was ready to chuck hers out the window. She'd taken classes and spent hours on end to learn basic computer skills because it was impossible to have any kind of decent job without knowing how to run one of the blasted machines.

The temp company she worked for had given her the position at the Anderson Corporate Offices and she'd been there for two months. It was a dream-come-true job and she hoped it would turn into a permanent position, because everyone knew employees of the Anderson's were loyal through and through. The Anderson's were great to their employee's, paid better wages than other corporations, offered great benefits, and were exceptionally family friendly.

She remained seated, arguing with her computer, grateful no one overheard her, because she was sure she sounded like an insane woman. By the time her lunch break came around she was about ready to cry. Her boss had slowly been adding more work, and she was sure it was a test, and if it was - she was failing miserably.

"Ms. Stellar, can you please go up to the top floor. The boss wants to talk to you," a voice asked over her intercom.

"Yes, I was getting ready for my lunch break, so I can head right up," she answered. Jennifer broke out in a cold sweat. She was going to lose her job. There was no other reason for her to be called up to the main offices. She'd never heard of anyone getting called up to Lucas Anderson's office. He was the President of the company and though she saw him regularly, walking around the floors, he never called anyone in her type of position to the corporate offices.

She didn't understand why he'd fire her personally, though. Normally, the guy in charge of her division would do that. She pushed the elevator button and waited nervously. She knew the computer projects had been a test, and her failure was unacceptable. She wasn't too proud to beg. She'd study day and night if that's what it took, because it wasn't only herself she had to think about.

***

"Are you sure she's the one?" George asked Joseph.

"Oh yes, I'm one hundred percent sure. I always take the time to know who's working here. Lucas took over as President years ago but I still like to handle personnel packages. I take a lot of pride knowing we offer more than other corporations. I especially check into temp employee's to deem whether or not they'll make a good fit for a permanent position. Jennifer is absolutely terrible when it comes to computers, but she's incredibly bright, eager, and willing to work hard," Joseph answered.

"How does that make her wife material, though?" George asked.

"Ah, you must let me finish," Joseph said. "She came to us through my favorite temp agency, and I did some research on her. She lost her sister six months ago to a drunk driver, which is especially tragic because her sister and brother-in-law had a child, who is four years old. It looks as if Jennifer has no other family, as her grandparents and parents have passed away."

"Where's the child?"

"Jennifer has been raising her since the accident, and I'm sure it's not easy for her. The little girl attends the on-site child care center, here," Joseph answered.

"Oh, this could mean an instant grandchild," George said in delight.

"I knew you'd be happy about that. Molly's a spitfire and too adorable for words. I've grown quite attached, since I spend a lot of time down there with her. My grandkids come in sometimes so they can play," Joseph told him.

"Ms. Stellar is here," the secretary told them over the intercom.

"Send her straight in," Joseph replied. Both men sat back and waited for Jennifer. When she opened the door, they could see the fear in her face, though she was doing a great job of trying to hide it. She looked surprised to see Joseph and George, instead of Lucas.

"Hello, Mr. Anderson. They said you needed to see me."

"Yes, thank you for coming, Ms. Stellar. Go ahead and have a seat," Joseph told her. "This is my brother, George Anderson. He's moving his corporate offices to Seattle and in need of a variety of new staff. One of those positions is for an executive administrator to the President and we would like to know if you might be interested. There would be a significant pay raise and added benefits."

Jennifer couldn't believe what she was hearing. She thought she was losing her job, and not only were they offering her a permanent position, but a better one, at that. She wanted to shout *yes*, but didn't know if she was truly qualified for the position. It would be terrible to get the new job, only to lose it for incompetence.

"I'm honored you would think of me. Yes, I'd be more than happy to accept the position, but I have to be honest with you. I'm struggling with the computer system I've been using. I can type about a hundred words a minute and do all basic computer functions, but the more complicated requests are giving me trouble. Please know, I'm more than willing to spend every spare minute I have to learn, though," she told them eagerly.

"Well, the great news is you won't have to deal with any programs you're currently using. You'll be typing a lot, and attending meetings, plus there's some travel involved," George told her.

Before Jennifer got too excited, she realized there was a problem. How could she travel? She had no one to watch Molly, and besides that, she couldn't take off for extended periods of time and leave her behind. Molly had already lost her parents and she was only recently able to cope with not seeing her mom and dad.

"We know you've recently taken on the responsibility of your niece and we're sorry about your loss. We have excellent programs here offering child care," Joseph said as if he could read her mind.

"How much would I have to be away?"

"On average, about three to five days a month," George said. *That wasn't too bad,* Jennifer reasoned. She'd be able to provide much better for her niece with the new position. She'd have money to buy the items she needed, and to afford to take her places, spending quality time together.

"I'll take it," she said with enthusiasm.

"That's great. You'll start next week, so for now you'll get a little time off - paid of course," George told her.

"Oh, I forgot to ask where the new offices are?" she questioned.

"They're going to be here. We've just purchased the building next door and will connect the buildings by creating a sky-bridge walkway. Until the construction is finished, they'll be using the twenty-second through twenty-fourth floors. You'll be stationed on the twenty-fourth so you can still use the daycare center, here," Joseph said.

"That's wonderful. Thank you for this opportunity," Jennifer told both men, shaking their hands briefly, then turning to make a quick exit.

Jennifer rode the elevator down to her floor and slowly walked into her office. She looked around in wonder. She'd gone up there dreading the worst and walked away feeling better than she had in six months.

"Congratulations, Ms. Stellar. I'm happy you received a promotion," her boss approached, sounding sincere.

"Thank you, Mr. Barry."

"I've enjoyed working with you, and we will miss having you as part of our team. If you want to place your possessions in boxes and label them, I can have them delivered to your new office. You don't have to worry about packing them home and back again," he offered.

"That would be great, thank you."

"No problem. When you're finished you can take the rest of the day off. Joseph told me the position was in effect immediately and he's already sent in for a temp," he said before leaving.

Jennifer hadn't brought too many personal items to work and it didn't take long to put her belongings in boxes. She was excited to pick up her niece early. With the beautiful weather, she'd be able to surprise Molly with an afternoon at the park.

Jennifer sat on a bench watching Molly play on the slide with a couple other kids. Molly had only just started sleeping through the night. Her poor niece had nightmares for months and Jennifer knew it was because she had abandonment issues, as any child would when their parents suddenly disappeared. Molly still had circles under her eyes, but not nearly as bad as they'd been a few months ago.

"Heads up," someone yelled. Just as Jennifer turned in the direction of the voice, she felt a pain in her neck and looked down in amazement at the frisbee lying next to her.

She brought her hand up and was surprised to feel a bit of blood. Whoever had thrown the thing, must have really chucked it.

"I'm sorry about that. Are you okay?" She looked up and lost her breath. Holy cow, the guy was stunning. To her surprise, her throat tightened and she struggled to get the words out. In the past, she never had trouble talking with attractive men, and she hadn't had that gut wrenching, stop-you-in-your-tracks response to a man since she was a teenager.

His dark hair was messy around his flushed cheeks. He had small drops of sweat dripping off of his forehead and the most piercing blue eyes she'd ever looked into. Her gaze followed a bead of sweat to his naked chest, quickening her heartbeat. The man had to be a model, with his defined chest and washboard abs. Even without flexing, the muscles in his arms were well defined. She followed his abs to his low-riding, athletic pants, before noticing her eyes had moved to an area she shouldn't be staring at.

Willing herself to obey, she jerked her eyes back up to his face, and watched as a cocky grin spread across his features, knowingly. He stood by silently as she ogled him. She stiffened her shoulders, irritated she'd been so immediately mesmerized by him. She hated to be another typical female, who thought only looks mattered. He was most likely some really stupid jock, who thought with a different head than the one on top of his shoulders. She realized she'd never answered him.

"I'm fine - I'm just glad you didn't hit any of the children," she stated and turned away, acting as if he wasn't there.

Trenton stared at the back of the striking, dark-haired stranger in a bit of shock. He was certainly used to the appraising look she'd given him, but not the suddenly dismissive attitude that followed. He was also not used to the immediate attraction he felt with her. She was not his typical type.

She couldn't have been much over five feet in height, and her dark brown hair and stunning green eyes were the opposite of the long-legged blondes with bigger chests than brains he normally went for. He could play with them and then walk away without anyone getting hurt over it.

He never picked up a woman in the park, as they were the commitment, till-death-do-us-part type and he would never take a trip down the aisle. He should count his blessings she was clearly not interested in him, but he'd hurt her, and couldn't leave until he knew she'd be okay.

"It looks like you might be bleeding. I'm going to look," he said as he bent next to her and moved her hair out of his way. He was relieved to only see a small cut, nothing needing stitches. The feel of her hair was surprisingly silky, and he suddenly had images of it spread out on his pillow.

Jennifer sucked in another breath from the feel of his warm touch. She about jumped out of the seat from the small movement of his fingers brushing against her neck. She passed it off as being overly tired.

"I'm fine, really," she said, needing him to remove his hands, since it was doing disturbing things to her stomach. She didn't have time for a man in her life, but if she did, it wouldn't be with a man like the guy before her. It would be with an average looking guy, who didn't stop women in their tracks.

"Wow, Trenton, you're only in town for a day and you're already attacking unsuspecting women." Jennifer glanced up as another handsome man joined their conversation, then looked down only to have her head whip back around as she realized it was Lucas Anderson. She'd never seen him wearing anything but expensive, tailored suits, and she could see why his wife was head-over-heels for him. Lucas was stunning, but while the other man made her stomach stir, Lucas did nothing physical for her. She figured it was because she knew he was married. Having met his wife several times, she knew how genuinely sweet she was, too.

"Well, you know how it is, any excuse to meet a sexy lady," Trenton answered and Jennifer felt her mouth drop open. No one ever referred to her as sexy, and she hated to admit his words made her glow a bit.

"You look familiar, and before you think that's some cheesy line, it's not. You really do look familiar," Lucas said. She had to clear her throat before she was able to speak clearly.

"I work for you, Mr. Anderson, or well I did until my promotion today. My name is Jennifer," she finally responded.

"That's right, I'm sorry. I'm so used to seeing everyone in the offices that out in a park setting throws me off," he told her with a heart-stopping grin.

"No problem, it took me a moment to recognize you, as well," she said with a genuine smile. He was an easy man to talk to, making her feel comfortable, unlike his companion.

"Hey, quit flirting - you're a married man," Trenton growled at Lucas. Jennifer felt her face flame with embarrassment.

"I… I wasn't flirting. I think your wife is wonderful," she stammered while sending a glare toward Trenton.

"Ignore him, Jennifer. He's just jealous because you obviously have better taste than to talk to an ogre like him," Lucas said with the same friendly smile. She was thankful for his words, causing her embarrassment to ease.

"Whatever, Lucas. You're lucky you're a married man, or I'd prove to you later all the ladies wouldn't even know you existed when we walked into a room together."

Jennifer watched the two of them rib each other and knew beyond a shadow of a doubt all the women in any room would be tripping over themselves to get to either of them. She was grateful she was too busy for relationships or she may have stood in line with them.

"I really am sorry about hitting you with the Frisbee. Why don't you give me your number so I can call and make sure you're okay later," Trenton said with the most seductive smile she'd ever witnessed. She had to call on some major willpower to deny him.

"I'll be fine, I promise. I have to leave, so you both have a great time," she said, blowing him off. She got up and walked to the other side of the playground, collected her niece, and quickly departed. She was angry with the heat she felt in her cheeks, and the way he'd made her stomach quiver. She had zero time for men and though a part of her wished she could've flirted back, she knew she'd done the right thing. Besides, she'd never see him again, anyway.

Trenton watched her walk away with a bit of shock. He'd never before been turned down by a female. He wasn't sure he liked the feeling. He usually had women stuffing their numbers in any available pocket he had, and yet the little spitfire of a woman he found both breathtaking and irritating at the same time, completely ignored him and walked away without so much as a backward glance.

"Oh, you just got burned badly, cousin. I guess Seattle women have better taste than those in Chicago."

"She has me intrigued. I'd chase her down, but luckily she works for your company, so I'll be able to find her," Trenton said, relishing the thought of her reaction when he did come in contact with her again.

"She said she was promoted and no longer worked for me. Heck, we didn't get her last name to even be able to find her," Lucas said.

"Oh, I'll find her alright. It's been a long time since a woman has peaked my interest like that," Trenton said. Lucas looked at his cousin with a huge grin. He knew that look well, as he and his brothers had all fought tooth and nail to hold onto their bachelorhood, only to end up chasing down their wives. His cousin was on the prowl, and Lucas almost felt sympathy for the mysterious Jennifer.

"Okay, well enough mooning over the girl, we're supposed to be having fun. You have to be back to work soon enough and we haven't spent nearly enough time together the last several years," Lucas told him. Trenton agreed, and they got back into their game. But the mysterious Jennifer stayed on his mind and Lucas kicked his butt all over the field. He was grateful when his brother Max showed up to help him out.

***

The Billionaire's Marriage Proposal is available at all major retailers.

ABOUT THE AUTHOR

Melody Anne is the author of the popular series, Billionaire Bachelors, and Baby for the Billionaire. She also has a Young Adult Series in high demand; Midnight Fire and Midnight Moon - Rise of the Dark Angel with a third book in the works called Midnight Storm.

As an aspiring author, she's written for years, then became published in 2011. Holding a Bachelor's Degree in business, she loves to write about strong, powerful, businessmen and the corporate world.

When Melody isn't writing, she cultivates strong bonds with her family and relatives and enjoys time spent with them as well as her friends, and beloved pets. A country girl at heart, she loves the small town and strong community she lives in and is involved in many community projects.

See Melody's Website at: www.melodyanne.com. She makes it a point to respond to all her fans. You can also join her on Facebook at: www.facebook.com/authormelodyanne, or at twitter: @authmelodyanne.

She looks forward to hearing from you and thanks you for your continued interest in her stories.

Manufactured by Amazon.ca
Bolton, ON

19163731R00176